Gold Diggers

THE SECRET OF BEAR MOUNTAIN

A novelization by Lisa Rojany

*Based on the motion picture
written by Barry Glasser*

Hippo

UNIVERSAL PICTURES PRESENTS A BREGMAN/DEYFILE PRODUCTION "GOLD DIGGERS THE SECRET OF BEAR MOUNTAIN" ANNA CHLUMSKY CHRISTINA RICCI POLLY DRAPER BRIAN KERWIN DIANA SCARWID DAVID KEITH COSTUME MARY McLEOD MUSIC JOEL McNEELY FILM EDITOR STEPHEN W. BUTLER PRODUCTION DESIGNER MICHAEL BOLTON DIRECTOR OF PHOTOGRAPHY ROSS BERRYMAN A.C.S. EXECUTIVE PRODUCER LOUIS A. STROLLER WRITTEN BY BARRY GLASSER PRODUCED BY MARTIN BREGMAN ROLF DEYFILE MICHAEL S. BREGMAN DIRECTED BY KEVIN JAMES DOBSON A UNIVERSAL RELEASE

Scholastic Children's Books,
Commonwealth House,
1-19 New Oxford Street
London WC1A 1NU, UK
a division of Scholastic Ltd
London ~ New York ~ Toronto ~ Sydney ~ Auckland

First published in USA by Price Stern Sloan, Inc., 1995
First published in the UK by Scholastic Ltd, 1995

Gold Diggers © copyright MCA Publishing Rights,
a division of MCA Inc.

ISBN 0 590 13662 3

Printed by Cox & Wyman Ltd, Reading, Berks.

10 9 8 7 6 5 4 3 2 1

Prologue

In her whole life, Beth Eastman had never met anyone quite like Jody Salerno. . . .

Beth hated leaving Los Angeles. She couldn't believe that her mother was moving them to small-town Wheaton, a little nowhere place past Seattle and tucked up close to the Canadian border. But when a family tragedy convinced her mother that they had to leave the city, nothing would change her mind. And Beth was perfectly prepared to hate every minute of that long, unbearable summer.

Then Beth met Jody. Jody was the girl who all the mothers despised. She was the kid the police always suspected when something went wrong in Wheaton. But Jody knew the secrets of the forest and mountains around them—she even had an idea where a legendary fortress of gold was hidden deep in the caves of Bear Mountain.

Together, the reluctant city girl and the ragtag country girl set out on an unforgettable summer adventure that would change their lives, and the lives of the townspeople, forever.

Chapter 1

The majestic mountain ranges of the Olympic Peninsula suddenly came into view. Miles and miles of lush, green rain forests were buried between its peaks. A rapidly flowing river snaked in and out of sight, the brilliant sunshine glittering off its constantly moving surface. Looking up into the clear blue sky, Beth Eastman suddenly longed for the smog-filled Los Angeles basin.

Why did they have to move at all? Beth wondered, feeling homesick and grim. Los Angeles had everything they needed. There were strip malls on every corner and bigger shopping malls where she and her friends loved to hang out. Restaurants and coffee shops were scattered all over the city. The Venice boardwalk was perfect for skating and people watching, not to mention all the vendors that sold cool earrings and funky shades. And it seemed that no other city had as many movie theaters as Los Angeles.

Beth already missed the packed summer beaches of

the Pacific Ocean, just a bus ride away from her old home. What was her mother, Kate, thinking when she decided to move them to some little, nowhere town in Washington state? Los Angeles had mountains, too. It even had a river, sort of. Los Angeles had everything! Everything Beth needed anyway.

Beth turned away from the passenger window of the sedan, which was packed with everything they owned. The trailer hitched behind them was filled with boxes, and rattled and bumped its way along the highway. "Are we there yet?" she asked.

"Beth, how could we be there?" replied her mother. "You know we're in the middle of nowhere."

"Isn't that where we're moving to—the middle of nowhere?" Beth said, slumping down in her seat and refusing to enjoy the lush greens of the scenery whizzing past her window.

Kate gritted her teeth. She'd been hearing her daughter complain for the last fifty miles. Beth knew her mother was trying to be patient with her.

But Beth also thought that if her mother was honest with herself, she'd admit to being nervous as well. Moving was scary. But, as she had told Beth right before they left, staying in the same city had become too difficult when Daddy had died. Everywhere Kate went in Los Angeles, she saw places where she and Beth's dad had been happy. Memories of their eleven years together as a family assaulted her from every direction. Beth's twelfth birthday had been so sad without her father, Kate could barely stand it. And if one more person looked at them with a face filled with sympathy and sent condolences, Kate thought she'd explode. What was there to be sorry for? Those years were the best years of their lives!

Her mother had insisted that regardless of what Beth said, moving was the best idea she'd had during this terrible year. They'd start a new life together, Kate had promised. They'd be happy. Happy happy happy, Beth chanted in her head. It was all a state of mind. Happy happy happy . . .

Her chanting wasn't working. "Maybe we're lost," Beth suggested.

"We're not lost," Kate answered, her hand reaching down to touch the creased state map, crushed because neither she nor Beth had been able to fold it back into its original dimensions.

"You always say you have no sense of direction," Beth offered cheekily.

"Don't be insulting."

"But we passed through Seattle *hours* ago," Beth complained. "Are you sure we're not lost?"

"I just told you—"

"Maybe I should drive . . ." said Beth, knowing her mother would never let her near the steering wheel.

"You're already driving me crazy!" said Kate.

Beth knew her mother was trying to be nice, even though she was trapped in a car with her twelve-year-old daughter who was making her insane.

"I was just trying to be helpful," Beth pouted. Kate was being too calm. She didn't like her mother so calm. It reminded Beth of that time after the funeral when her mother had walked around like a zombie for months. Beth had thought she'd die from sadness, too, but at least she hadn't gone crazy and decided to move them practically to Canada.

Beth missed her dad so much, she could still conjure up the sound of his voice booming through the house when he came home from classes. He and her mom would talk in the kitchen every night about his students and the crazy things they said and wrote in their papers. He had been a history professor, with every summer off to spend with the family. For as long as Beth could remember, the three of them had driven all over the country on family trips. He would take out library books about each state, and they would visit all the famous places, her dad telling them stories throughout the entire trip.

He had been very proud that Beth could recite the capitals of every state by the time she was six years old. At ten, she had toured thirty-six states. Maybe that's why they were moving to Washington. That was one place the three of them had never visited together, even though Kate had spent a great deal of time there as a child. Maybe her mother would decide to leave at the end of the summer after all, Beth hoped, crossing her fingers.

The sedan suddenly drove over a large hole in the road, rattling the trailer behind them. Beth turned around to make sure it was still attached to the car. With all their stuff packed behind them, it sure didn't feel like a summer vacation.

"Relax and enjoy the scenery," Kate said, noticing the worried look on Beth's face. "Isn't it beautiful?"

"It's too quiet," Beth snapped.

"It would be if you'd shut the—" Kate stopped herself just in time, "—if you'd just stop talking."

Beth gasped in mock horror. Nabbed! "You almost used the f-word!"

"I know," said Kate, already regretting the slip.

"My own mother," Beth said, shaking her head back and forth in exaggerated disbelief.

"I'm never going to hear the end of this, am I?" Kate said, glancing over at Beth through the corner of her eye.

"Nope."

"I suppose you're going to really enjoy torturing me with it until we get to Wheaton, aren't you?" Kate said, smiling despite herself.

"Yep." The car was silent.

"You little brat!" said Kate, grinning.

Beth gasped again, shaking her finger at her mother like a grown-up would to a naughty little kid. Kate reached over and tousled Beth's hair. Beth knew she was a funny kid. And Kate was usually grateful to have a daughter with a sense of humor.

"So, are we there yet?" Beth asked.

Kate's right arm shot over to the passenger side, her hand clamping shut over Beth's mouth. Forget being grateful. Who needed a kid with a sense of humor anyway?

Chapter 2

Hours later Beth and her mother were driving through a lovely, quiet street in the heart of Wheaton.

Tall wooden framed houses, dating back to the early 1900s, lined the street. Each well-kept house had a long, green, perfectly manicured lawn leading from the street to the porch. On practically every porch that Beth saw, a rocking chair sat or a hanging bench swung slightly in the breeze. Each house had shuttered windows painted to match little picket fences or tall front doors. Enormous oak trees rose from lawns and street sides, blanketing the street with shade and leaf-shaped shadows. Even though it was summer, the air felt crisp and cool.

"Isn't it glorious?" sighed Kate, transported by her idea of the perfect suburban dream.

Beth didn't think it was all that glorious. Where were the people? The streets were totally deserted. Even the cars parked in the driveways and carports seemed abandoned to her. Los Angeles had suburbs that were as quiet as this, but they didn't seem so . . . so cute. Who wanted to live in a cute place where the only thing you could hear was the rustling of the trees?

Kate flicked the turn signal and the car swung into a driveway. She turned off the engine and they got out of the car. She stretched, taking huge gulps of fresh air into her lungs, while Beth sniffed at the air. Too clean. She missed the smog.

"Every summer when I got to come here, my Aunt Alice would be waiting for me right there on the porch with a big pitcher of lemonade," Kate said, "and a plate of piping hot, homemade muffins."

Give me a break, thought Beth. Everyone knew muffins were filled with fat and sugar. What was her mother thinking? "Mom," she said, "I think you've really lost it."

Beth glanced back at the house. It looked like every other house on the street. She was suddenly filled with a sense of dread and loneliness. This wasn't home. Once she went in the house she'd feel as if she was committing to staying there. She turned her back to the front door and toward the oak-lined street, looking up and down in either direction. "So, Mom, where's the mall?"

Her mother gave her an exasperated look and put her hands on her hips. Kate stared at the house and then back at the packed car and trailer filled with all their earthly belongings. They had a lot of work ahead of them. Kate was determined to make this old house into a home.

Later that day, Beth and her mother had managed to unload the entire trailer and most of the contents of the car. A trail of boxes lined the driveway from the back of the empty trailer up to the front door.

Inside, the house looked like something right out of a movie about people summering in New England. Aunt Alice's furniture was old but solid, some of it covered with sheets. As Beth looked around again, she had the eerie feeling that someone still lived there, even though Aunt Alice was long gone. Dusty knick-knacks still lined the fireplace mantel and side tables, on which rested framed photographs of people Beth had never met before. The floor rugs looked musty and the air smelled old.

Upstairs, Beth opened the door to her new room. A fine mist of dust rose into the air, illuminated by a shaft of light from the picture window. The room had a view of the front lawn with an old oak tree conveniently located just within reach outside the window. Perfect for climbing down, but of course she didn't mention that to her mother, who was downstairs dressed in already-filthy work clothes, trying to create some order out of the chaos of their stuff lying all over the place.

Beth jumped down the stairs two at a time and decided to try setting up the television. She plugged it in and turned it on. But no matter how many times and in how many configurations she bent and rotated the TV antenna, the reception looked muddy and the voices faded in and out, chopping up the sound so that it was nearly unintelligible.

"Great. Two channels," Beth complained. "And you can't get either one of them." Living in this house was going to be miserable. Hadn't old Aunt Alice ever heard of cable? Beth tried to imagine Aunt Alice. What came to mind was a bonneted country woman, a crocheted shawl draped over thin shoulders, knitting sweaters in front of the television while watching quiz shows and soap operas. Aunt Alice probably *liked* all this peace and quiet.

Kate walked over to the exasperated Beth. "You don't want to watch television," she said, ushering her to the front door. "Go ahead, honey, I'll finish your room. Go outside, get to know the neighborhood."

Beth made her way carefully around the stacks of opened boxes and out to the porch. Her bicycle rested against the railing. She hopped on and headed in the general direction that her mom had pointed out as the center of town.

She passed a sign: WHEATON, WASHINGTON. POPULATION 6,240. Great, she thought to herself, junior high schools in Los Angeles had almost that many people. All of a sudden the road widened slightly and she found herself in a tiny little town. She felt as if she were in munchkinland, cycling past a small brick court house, a tiny library next to a sheriff's station, and finally, a post office, all tucked into a neat little town square.

Near the post office she saw two people milling about outside. She whizzed up to them and braked to a screeching halt. One of them jumped.

"Excuse me," Beth said, "where's the mall?"

The couple looked at her like she was crazy. "The what?" said one. They had no idea what she was talking about! Were they from another planet?

Beth tried to smile a thanks as she hopped back on the pedals and zoomed away. Soon she discovered a business district, of sorts, with a real estate office so small it had instant pictures of various properties taped up to its front window. A professional building was followed by a bank so quaint that Beth half expected a stagecoach to drive up to it and cowboys wearing black masks and spurs to jump out and announce a stick-up.

Beth pumped to the top of a hill and then whizzed down, popping a wheelie as she skidded to a halt at the bottom, spraying gravel to the side of the bike. Then she headed down Main Street. Every place she had ever been to had a Main Street, even Los Angeles; this thought filled her with hope as she passed some tiny boutiques and a 1950s diner with stools at the counter and an old soda fountain.

Suddenly she heard a commotion across the street. Voices yelling. It was a fight! Two boys were circling another kid. The kid threw sharp jabs at both boys, bobbing and weaving like a professional boxer and making contact every time. Beth watched as the kid faked a turn then dived, butting them both in the chest and sending them reeling to the sidewalk.

But wait! The kid who had just downed the two boys was not another boy, it was a girl! She fought better than any girl Beth had ever seen! Before the two boys could struggle to their feet much less chase her, the girl was already halfway down the block.

Beth watched in fascination. She could hardly make out the girl's face that moments before had been scrunched up in determination. So there *were* kids in this nowhere town after all! Beth's eyes followed the racing girl around the corner and across an empty field. She ran like an athlete, smooth and fast, disappearing out of sight.

Beth rode in the general direction the girl had fled, hoping she knew something Beth didn't about the cool places to go in this town. Beth was beginning to doubt there were any cool places. She reached the top of another hill that overlooked all of Wheaton. The town below her looked so tiny and insignificant. So infinitely boring.

Beth sighed. "We left L.A. for this?" She couldn't believe her misfortune.

Chapter 3

The next morning, the sun streamed in Beth's window, but still she slept. The silence was suddenly pierced with the loudest—and only—COCK-A-DOODLE-DO that Beth had ever heard.

She jumped up from beneath the sheets and groaned. "Oh, no." She squinted into the morning light, whisking the sheets back up over her head.

Kate sat up, bursting with energy. "Let's go," she chirped. "Up and at 'em!" Kate gave Beth a little shove, causing her daughter to sit up reluctantly.

Beth's room was in total disarray. Cartons lay everywhere. Clothes were piled in corners, waiting to be hung up and stacked in drawers. She and her mother had decided to share the bed the first night. Kate had insisted it was to make Beth sleep better, but Beth suspected it was the other way around.

"I can't believe it. I heard a rooster crow!" Beth exclaimed, suddenly feeling starved. "I'm used to hearing traffic. I miss traffic. And bad air. And my friends,

Mom. I miss my friends. I'll probably never be able to make new ones."

Kate looked at her daughter. The poor kid. Kate sat back down on the bed and drew Beth tightly into a loving hug.

"Oh yes you will, baby," she said reassuringly. "Remember our deal. We'll try it out for the summer and see how it goes. But you won't want to leave." She pulled Beth closer to her. "Beth, it's scary for me, too, without your father. Sometimes I feel like I'm walking across one of those old, wobbly suspension bridges without anything to hang on to. But we'll hang on to each other. C'mon. OK?"

Beth snuggled closer to her mom. "OK, Mom," she agreed. She felt a little bit better knowing her mom wasn't as set on this place as she pretended to be. Maybe she'd try a little harder to make it better for both of them. Truth was, Beth was getting a little bit tired of being grumpy all the time anyway.

By lunchtime, Beth and her mom were starved and sick of eating all the ready-made foods they'd been munching for days on their road trip. Beth left her mom still cleaning and hopped on her bicycle, heading for the market.

On the way home, she kept reaching over her handlebars to prevent the grapefruit on the top of the bag from slipping out of the basket altogether. She was riding down a mountain trail in the hills above Wheaton. And she was speeding along very fast. As she rode around a blind curve, she lost control of the bike and flew off the main road onto the slope of a forest clearing.

The grapefruit was forgotten as Beth careened downhill through a maze of tree stumps, hanging on to the handlebars for dear life. Her wild descent was taking her directly in the path and on a certain collision course with a girl halfway downhill. Lurching over a stump, all Beth could see was that the girl had slung over her shoulder what looked like a homemade fishing pole. Was that the same girl she had seen beat up the two boys the day before?

Hearing the whirr of Beth's bicycle, the girl turned around and spotted Beth hurling directly toward her. The bike was getting closer and it was clear that Beth was out of control.

The girl tried to dodge by zigging out of the way, but Beth zigged, too. Whenever the girl zagged, Beth zagged, too.

"I can't stop! Get out of the way!" cried Beth, her voice sounding bubbly from all the bumps she was speeding over.

The girl darted through the open door of a storage shack to escape, but Beth plowed right through the same door. The girl raced out the other side with Beth in reluctant pursuit. From the opened door, the shack's contents came streaming out behind the two girls—dozens of rubber tires were picking up speed down the hill, threatening to plow them over.

Looming in front of Beth were the banks of a running creek. Just as Beth was about to run her over, the other girl tossed aside her fishing pole and dove into the water. Milliseconds later, Beth finally laid on the brakes and flew off the bike seat, over the handlebars, and straight into the water. Every last one of the bouncing tires jumped up onto the banks and boinged straight in the water after them.

When the last of the tires had submerged, the scene was a wreck. For a moment there was no sound but the gurgle of the rushing creek water. Beth's bicycle lay on its side, halfway in the water with the front wheel still spinning. Sopped groceries lay scattered about. One lone tire was plopped on the bank.

Then up from the creek popped the strange girl's head. Up came Beth, too. Both were sputtering and coughing out water like a couple of choking seals. Each girl wiped the water out of her eyes before she realized they were both dog-paddling face to face!

"Who are you? Evel Knievel?" exploded the girl.

"Are you OK?" said Beth. "I'm sorry. . . ."

The strange girl slogged up toward the banks of the creek, muttering. "It's a miracle I'm still alive!" Her voice sounded less than nice. "At least I think I am!"

"Oh, gosh, I'm sorry," Beth repeated.

At that moment, the strange girl grabbed her ankle in agony. To Beth's horror, she stumbled and staggered onto the bank, clutching the right side of her body, first her leg, then her thigh, then her shoulder, screaming, "Agggghhh! Oh, my goodness!"

Beth waded up to the shore in a rush. "What's wrong . . . uh . . . what's your name?"

"Jody, if it's any business of yours. Jody Salerno," she gasped. "The pain, it's awful. I'll have to see my lawyer. I may decide to sue."

Beth frowned. "You don't look like you're hurt," she said, looking Jody up and down.

"It takes twenty-four hours for bruises to show," Jody stated matter-of-factly. "Tomorrow I'll look like an eggplant." She rubbed her shoulder. "This could cost you major dollars."

"I said I was sorry," Beth replied contritely. "Twice."

"Sorry doesn't count in court," Jody replied nastily. She continued to massage her shoulder, when she seemed to realize something and stopped short. "My camera! I was wearing it around my neck!" Jody stalked up and down the bank of the creek, her shoes making a squelching sound, looking in vain for the missing camera. "My beautiful, expensive, twelve-hundred-dollar Nikon 326 that I saved up forever to buy. And you're gonna have to pay me back!"

Beth suddenly became suspicious. Was this girl pulling her leg or what? "I didn't see you wearing a camera," she stated evenly.

"Well, I was!"

"I'm not giving you a single, solitary cent," vowed Beth heatedly.

"I'll see you in court!" spat Jody.

Beth threw Jody a disgusted look. "Fine," she said, beginning to gather up the soggy groceries. "The name's Eastman. Beth. Just try to get me to court."

Jody was silent for a moment. "Relax," she finally said, "I'm not suing you."

"I knew that," said Beth, pausing as she looked at Jody, the muddy grapefruit in her hand.

"No you didn't," said Jody. "I had you squirming."

"Just how dumb do you think I am?" asked Beth. She'd watched lots of TV shows. She knew what was up. Who was this redneck country girl to try to trick *her*, the wise city girl?

"Dumb enough to let a lizard crawl up your leg," said Jody calmly.

Beth went berserk, screaming and jumping, stomping her feet to free the creepy crawler—which didn't exist. She'd been had.

"And apparently dumb enough to look!" stated

Jody triumphantly.

"Eeeeuuuu!" Beth was furious. How humiliating to have fallen for such an easy trick.

"Eeeeuuuu!" mimicked Jody, grabbing her fishing pole and starting off.

When Beth tried to walk away with her bike, she noticed that it had a flat tire. The spokes of one wheel were completely mangled. She groaned. This was just about the very last straw. Beth dumped the remaining groceries into the battered basket and started dragging the bike up the hill—the opposite direction from Jody.

Just as she approached the top of the hill, she peeked a look in Jody's direction. Jody was peeking right back. Both girls whirled back around and marched off, each going her separate way.

Chapter 4

While Beth was limping home with her wrecked bike, Kate was having the time of her life back at the house. She sat on the porch with her new friend and neighbor, Grace Briggs, and Grace's daughter, Tracy, who just happened to be Beth's age.

Kate was excited that Beth might be able to make a friend their second day in Wheaton, and she wolfed down a huge slice of the homemade pie Grace had so graciously brought over as a welcome-to-the-neighborhood present.

"Mmmm! Oh, Grace," praised Beth's mom, "this is so delicious, it's sinful. I'm going to gain thirty pounds living next door to you."

Kate looked over at her new friend. Even though Grace Briggs was a tiny bit pretentious, she was terrific company. And Tracy seemed like a nice kid—maybe a little stuck up. But perhaps that was just shyness at meeting a new grown-up.

Grace cut a slice of pie for herself. "It's third generation, my grandmother's recipe. With one or two of my special secrets." She gave Kate a mock secret wink.

"I'd kill for those secrets," Kate replied. "This was so nice of you to go to all this trouble."

"That's how we do things here."

Kate smiled. "Yes, I remember. . . ." she said, as if the taste of the pie took her back twenty years to her childhood. She turned to Tracy. "I can't wait for you to meet Beth."

"She sounds wonderful," Grace said when Tracy did not respond. "They're going to be great friends. Tracy will show her around and introduce her to everybody, won't you, sweetheart?"

Just then Beth headed up the driveway, dragging her crippled bicycle at her side. She removed the sopping bag of groceries from the basket and stomped onto the porch.

Kate, Grace, and Tracy stared at her in disbelief. She was dripping wet, soaked from head to toe, and muddy to boot.

"I live in L.A. my whole life, not one single accident. I'm here two days and my bicycle is wrecked, I almost drown, and I get threatened with a lawsuit by a hillbilly! A day in the country starring Beth Eastman." She dropped the sodden bag of groceries onto Kate's lap, looking completely disgusted.

"Honey," said her mother, "I'd like you to meet—"

"Hello, hello, and hello," Beth said to all three of them and marched into the house, the screen door slamming behind her.

Kate didn't know what to say. How could she even begin to help her daughter make friends when all Beth did was be rude to the first people who were nice to them?

Tracy looked at the screen door and burst out laughing. She was bored. Might as well hear the whole story straight from the horse's mouth. She got up and followed Beth into the house.

There were dozens and dozens of them everywhere. Bright, plump, luscious berries simply bursting from the bushes. Beth couldn't eat enough of them. They tasted nothing like the bitter ones at home that were so rare and expensive.

"Mmmm." Beth smacked her lips. This day just might end not so badly after all.

Tracy had dragged Beth and another friend of hers, Samantha, out to the field to pick berries. Samantha was all right, but a little bit too boy crazy, as far as Beth was concerned.

"The mall's about forty-five minutes from here, and even when we can't get rides from our parents, there's a bus that goes there," said Samantha.

"Great," said Beth. "At least we're not completely stranded." Beth dropped some more berries into her pail on the ground. She moved along a row of bushes to pick more. "I can't believe anyone can just come out here and take these," she marveled.

"You're really into this," said Tracy. Beth was the first real city girl that had ever moved to Wheaton for good. Most of the other city girls just summered there. Tracy and her friends had been berry picking since they were little kids. It was no biggie.

Beth turned to drop some more berries in her pail. But where was it? She finally found the pail a few bushes down—but it was a lot farther away than Beth thought she had left it. I'm going crazy already, Beth thought, imagining headlines back home in the *Los Angeles Times*: GIRL KIDNAPPED TO COUNTRY BY MOTHER. GOES INSANE FROM POISONOUS BERRIES. NEWS AT ELEVEN.

Samantha interrupted her thoughts. "I'm dying to go to L.A.," she said. "All those beach parties, it must be so cool. Do you guys start dating when you're like nine down there?"

"Date? Me?" said Beth. "No! Do you date?"

"My mother would kill me," said Samantha, frowning as if she couldn't believe how unreasonable her mother was.

Beth picked more berries and started back to her

pail. But the pail was gone! Beth scratched her head, then looked at Tracy and Samantha. Neither one seemed to notice anything weird.

"When do we start dating?" asked Samantha.

"Eighth grade," said Tracy with authority. "That's when you start shaving under your arms. But I'm not going to."

"Date or shave under your arms?" asked Samantha.

"Men don't shave under there, so why should we?" replied Tracy. "Italian women don't either."

Samantha looked totally shocked. "I'm not having hairy pits. Guys hate it if you have hairy pits—"

Beth, circling the field, interrupted her, "Did you see my pail? I left it right over there. It's—gone!"

"Is that it over there?" asked Tracy, pointing.

Somehow the pail had moved to where it now rested under a grove of trees—all the way across the field. Beth shook her head and headed toward the pail. When she reached down, the branches of the tree shook, and all sorts of junk—an old shoe, dirt, leaves, tin cans, and the like—came tumbling down all over her. She covered her head.

When the barrage ended, a roaring peal of laughter began. Beth looked up. Sitting on a tree limb, laughing her head off, was Jody. Her laugh sounded like a cross between a hiccough and a donkey bray.

"Oh great. The redneck," Beth said to herself.

Then she said loud enough for Jody to hear, "You must be in pretty good shape to climb up there—especially with a busted shoulder!" Now Jody really couldn't sue her. Jody's story would fall apart in court when she came to the part where she climbed a tall tree mere hours after her life-threatening injuries.

Beth picked up her pail, about to leave. Even though she was itchy from the dirt that had rained from above, there was no way she'd show it by wiping it off. She'd just completely ignore that it had happened, that way Jody would get no satisfaction from a trick well played.

"Don't!" cried Jody, pointing at Beth's berry laden pail. "Don't eat those berries. You'll get sick."

Beth sensed another trap. For a minute she wasn't sure whether to ignore Jody or reply. And all those berries she'd already eaten. . . . But the thought of some foreign country disease getting her sick won out. "There's nothing wrong with them," Beth finally said.

"These are OK," said Jody. "Those are the ones that are bad."

"Which?"

"Those."

"Which are these and which are those?" asked Beth, waving her hands in the air.

"Those are these and these are those," replied Jody.

Beth couldn't believe what she was hearing.

" 'Those are these and these are those?' " she repeated, her voice rising.

Jody began to quote a *Winnie the Pooh* poem.

All of a sudden, Beth remembered. Her Dad had loved this poem, too. Beth quoted the next line.

The two girls studied each other, suspicion and dislike fading just a tad.

"You know *Winnie the Pooh?*" asked Beth.

"I read it with my dad a long time ago," said Jody.

"So did I. With my dad," said Beth. All of a sudden, Beth started to like Jody—a little. She couldn't be all that bad if she quoted one of Beth's favorite poems, now could she?

At that exact instant, Jody must have been thinking the same thing, that Beth wasn't all that bad, for she swung from the high limb to a lower limb then landed on the ground with a small "oomph!" Hands on hips and head held high standing right in front of Beth, Jody looked like she was ready for more.

They traded reciting the poem aloud, line by line, until Beth made a mistake.

"No, no, no," corrected Jody. " 'What'! It's 'what is who.' "

" 'What'?"

"That's right! 'What'!"

"No. 'Which.' "

" 'What'!"

" 'Which'!"

" 'What'!"

Tracy and Samantha appeared outside the grove. They watched Beth and Jody yelling. What in the heck was going on with those two?

" 'Which'!"

" 'What'!"

"OK. 'What.' " Beth gave in.

Jody was caught off guard. " 'What'?"

"Yes. 'What.' " Beth said simply.

Then Beth and Jody erupted into peals of laughter, each girl poking the other in the ribs. Tracy and Samantha looked dumbfounded. What was this new girl doing with Jody, the gutter rat? No one liked Jody. She was a troublemaker. It was better for Beth if she got away from Jody. And now.

Tracy shouted, "Beth, come on. We have to go."

"What are you? Her mother?" Jody shouted back.

"No, Jody, her friend," replied Tracy. "Something you wouldn't know anything about."

Jody moved toward Tracy as if to pick a fight, but held herself back. "You're not worth it," she mumbled under her breath. To Beth, she said, "Come on, let's get out of here." Jody started off, then stopped and waited for Beth to follow.

"Beth! Wait a minute, we should talk!" said Tracy, beckoning Beth over to her and Samantha. Where she belonged. Not with that trashy girl.

Together, Tracy and Samantha started to explain to Beth. "That's Jody Salerno."

"She's totally trashy."

"Bad news."

"She steals."

"She fights with everyone."

"She's always getting people into trouble."

"She's never in school; she always gets left back."

"She lies about everything."

"Her mother's a boozer."

"No one ever goes to her house. Not even Jody."

"I hear she sleeps in the woods."

"She's dangerous!"

Beth had heard more than enough. It was bad enough that they were tattletales, but these two girls were totally trashing Jody. And Jody couldn't be all that bad if she could quote A. A. Milne's *Winnie the Pooh* by heart, now could she?

"I appreciate the warning," Beth said to Samantha and Tracy. No need to make enemies. "And thanks for showing me the berries! See you later!" Beth grabbed her pail and headed into the woods after Jody.

Samantha and Tracy looked at each other, stunned. "You heard it here first!" Tracy called out to Beth's back. "You better be careful!"

Chapter 5

The pail heavy at her side, Beth finally caught up to Jody. The other girl yelled a thundering, "Whoaaaaaaaaa!"

Seconds later, Jody was hanging from a rope attached to an overhanging tree and swinging across a gorge over the creek. Beth stopped at the edge of the cliff and looked down. The distance between the two cliffs looked enormous to Beth. The drop to the flowing water of the creek was incalculable. Vertigo. Yuck.

Jody swung to the other side and landed with room to spare. "Yes, ma'am!" she cried triumphantly as she swung the rope back across the gorge to Beth. "Your turn."

"Nope. Forget it," said Beth. There was no way. No possible way.

"What's the matter, city girl? Are you scared?" taunted Jody.

"No!"

"Oh, yes you are. . . ."

"I am not!" retorted Beth, lying.

"You are, too," said Jody, knowing full well Beth was lying.

Beth dumped the pail. "Am . . . NOOOOOT . . ." cried Beth. She ran backward, then grabbed the rope, took a sprinting leap, and sailed across the gorge. But she didn't quite make it, landing just beneath the cliff on a rocky slope. She quickly grabbed onto some brush, which immediately came loose. She started to panic as she fell back.

Jody reached down and grasped her hand, pulling Beth over the top. Beth stood back from the edge and looked down. They were really high up there. Beth and Jody slapped a high-five! Beth couldn't believe her sudden change in fortune. She was finally having some real fun!

That weekend, Kate went on another crazed sanitary streak. After a week she was still scrubbing the house. After all their stuff had been unpacked—in record time—she had started with the downstairs rooms, washing the floors on hands and knees, scrubbing the walls, dusting the dirty windows. Then she attacked the upstairs. Carpets had been beaten, bathrooms were whipped into a sparkle of white, even Beth's room looked strangely germ-free. And yet Kate wasn't done. After all, the downstairs might have a speck of dirt somewhere that she had forgotten.

Beth had never seen her mother act like such a clean freak. Was this behavior a precursor to that disease where people couldn't stop washing their hands over and over and over? Beth hoped not. The smell of cleaning fluids was probably just temporarily making her mother act bizarre. She'd have to run out of them sometime soon.

Beth bounded down the stairs and sat at the bottom step to tie her sneakers. She watched her mother, still going at the floors on her hands and knees.

Kate sat up on her haunches, wiping her sweaty forehead with the back of her hand and sighing. "Look at you," she said to Beth. "Less than a week ago you were convinced you'd never make any friends. Now you're out the door again. Where are you off to?"

Beth looked at her mom in surprise. Beth was always up front about where she was going and when she'd be back. Ever since her dad had died, they had made an agreement to keep each other informed about the other's whereabouts. But her mom sounded weird. Almost as if she didn't trust her. Or was Kate just sad and lonely herself?

"To meet Jody," Beth replied, frowning. "I thought you were going to start working on your book."

"I have to get the floors done first," said Kate. "What happened to Tracy and Samantha?"

Beth got up to leave. "They don't get along with Jody. But they're wrong. I like her, there's something about her. Besides, she knows *Winnie the Pooh*."

"Oh well," said Kate, going back to her never-ending cleaning, "she can't be all that bad then." But Beth didn't hear her. She was already gone.

Half an hour later, Jody and Beth were horsing around in a beautiful clearing in the woods. Wispy grass grew high above their waists, sometimes taller than their heads. Jody was holding Beth by the ankles, swinging her around faster and faster and faster. They were both laughing and screaming. Finally both girls collapsed in happy exhaustion.

They agreed that their stomachs were growly and in serious need of some nutrition. They walked into town to the convenience store, where they bought a big bag of cookies to share. So engrossed were the girls in talking to each other that neither of them noticed the pickup truck pulling up behind them.

"Jody!" a woman shouted from the truck.

Jody and Beth both turned at the same time. "It's my mother," said Jody in a whisper to Beth, "and her boyfriend."

Beth studied Lynette Salerno. She sported a simple summer dress that made her look pretty and girlish. But she was wearing too much makeup, the lipstick and pancake foundation looking a little too orangey bright for good taste.

Ray Karnisak, Lynette's boyfriend, was a handsome guy who looked just a bit younger than Beth's father had been. He had a rugged, outdoorsy look to him and when he smiled, he was all charm.

Ray leaned out the truck window and spoke to Jody. "Hi. I'm taking your mother out for dinner at River Point. Do you wanna come?"

Jody said nothing. Beth wondered why she was being so quiet.

"Your friend can come, too," added Ray.

He sounded friendly enough to Beth, so why was Jody hanging back?

Lynette finally spoke. "Ray, honey, these kids don't want to sit in a stuffy ol' restaurant. Jody's having fun with her friend." Lynette was looking straight at Beth with her eyebrows raised and an expectant smile on her face.

Beth got it. She reached up to the truck to shake hands. "I'm Beth Eastman. I'm very pleased to meet you." Beth shook hands with both Lynette and Ray.

"Well, thank you!" said Lynette, obviously surprised at Beth's good manners.

Well, what did she expect? Beth wondered.

Ray smiled at the girls and said to Lynette, "Look at these two—they're ready to catch lightnin' in a bottle!"

"Have a good time now, girls," said Lynette, waving as the truck pulled away. Beth figured that Lynette was happier anyway, being able to share a dinner alone with her boyfriend without two kids getting in the way of a romantic evening.

"They're nice," Beth said to Jody. Jody didn't say anything. Beth read the bumper sticker on the truck as it drove away: SHOOT AN OWL, SAVE A LOGGER.

"Is he a logger?" Beth asked Jody.

"He ain't an owl," said Jody, immediately falling silent again.

They continued down the street, Beth wondering what was up with her new friend. "Does he live with you?" Beth asked.

"No, but he comes over a lot."

"What about your dad?" pressed Beth, wincing a little at the word dad. She still had a hard time believing she didn't have one anymore.

"He died. When I was seven," Jody stated, looking at the sidewalk.

Beth couldn't believe it. "So did mine. Last year."

Jody's head lifted and the two girls stared at each other. It was an unusual and sad thing to have in common, being fatherless. It made Beth somehow feel closer to Jody. Beth handed Jody some cookies and they kept walking.

"Does your mother have a boyfriend?" asked Jody.

"No," Beth sighed, "it's too soon for her." Her mother had said it enough to make Beth believe it. Who could understand adults anyway?

"Do you think she misses it?" asked Jody.

Beth looked at her, confused.

"*It*, you know . . ." explained Jody.

"Oh! Yeah. They always miss it, don't they?" Beth laughed and the two girls bumped each other, making Beth nearly trip. "Why do you think grown-ups make such a big deal out of it?"

"Probably because you have to get naked," Jody said with confidence. "Did you ever see a guy naked? Babies don't count."

Beth thought for only a second. "No. Did you?"

"In the movies."

"A PG?"

"No, an R."

"How did you get in?" asked Beth. She would bet in a second that tricks like that were easy for Jody, Miss I'm-Not-Afraid-of-Anything.

"It was a drive-in. I watched the movie through a pair of binoculars."

"Cool. Can we go?" asked Beth.

"They tore it down," said Jody.

"Were they doing it? In the movie?"

"No," replied Jody. "But I think people in the audience were."

Beth suddenly felt out of it. She'd never seen any-one doing it. She was supposed to be this sophisticated city girl, but Jody seemed to have had a lot more adventures than Beth ever had back home.

The two girls ambled out of Wheaton's main square, heading down the road. Every once in a while Beth would cross over into Jody's path, and Jody would bump Beth's hip with her own to keep her on her side. Beth did the same back. They chewed on long blades of grass, cupping them in their palms so Jody could teach Beth how to make them whistle.

Beth removed the grass from her mouth. "What do people do around here for excitement?"

"They move somewhere else," said Jody.

"My mother loves it here. She says it's better for her work," stated Beth.

"What does she do?"

"She's writing a children's book about an ostrich who gets lost. A lostrich." Beth groaned. It sure sounded dumb when she said it out loud. Did her mother really think kids wanted to hear about a lost animal that most kids had never set eyes on? Maybe her mother knew some interesting fact about ostriches that Beth didn't.

Jody rolled her eyes in reply. "Sorry there isn't more to do—except for tomorrow, of course."

"What's tomorrow?"

"June 21st," Jody said coyly.

Beth gave Jody a duh-you're-so-funny look. "What's so special about June 21st?"

"Sorry, Eastman, I'm not sure I can trust you." With a laugh, Jody slipped off the road and into the trees, picking up speed. Beth ran after her, catching up after a few long strides.

"You're faking me out, right? Nothing's happening tomorrow," Beth half-asked, half-stated.

"It just happens to be the first day of summer. And the longest day of the year. The summer solstice!"

"So?" Beth still didn't figure there was anything so special about that. It wasn't like it was the Fourth of July or anything. No one had summer solstice parties that she knew of.

"So," said Jody, "at high noon we can be rich!"

"How?"

"Billionaires, Eastman. Trillionaires, even. That's all I can tell you for now," Jody said mysteriously, "except that this will be the greatest adventure you'll ever have. Meet me tomorrow morning outside the elementary school on Dogwood and Third at 7:30. Sharp!" With that, Jody ran away, back toward what Beth assumed was her house.

Beth stood there, staring at Jody's rapidly receding back. Just what on earth did Jody mean? How could the summer solstice make them rich?

Well, Beth thought, I guess I'll find out tomorrow. An adventure might liven up this sleepy little town. It sounded great. Beth could hardly wait!

Chapter 6

At 7:30 sharp the next morning, Beth was at the elementary school, waiting patiently. She had barely been able to sleep, wondering just what Jody had meant about an adventure worth millions of dollars. The minutes ticked by. Still Beth waited. Where was Jody?

Just as she started to feel a riffle of annoyance, a police car cruised to a stop in front of her. It was Matt Hollinger, Wheaton's town sheriff. He looked to be about her mother's age. Beth thought he was kind of cute, for an old guy.

"Can I help you?" Matt asked.

"I'm waiting for someone," Beth said.

"Mind if I ask who?" said Matt.

"Jody Salerno."

"And Jody's late, huh?"

Beth nodded. This guy was so laid back, and Beth was taken by surprise. Cops in Los Angeles were usually much more businesslike. They didn't generally cruise by in their big cars just to chat with little girls who weren't causing any trouble.

"Did you check her house?" asked Matt.

Beth suddenly realized that she didn't know where Jody lived. She told Matt so.

"Hop in," Matt offered. "I'll take you."

Matt drove her to the outskirts of town, where the houses were lined up like a bunch of makeshift bungalows. The nearby woods seemed to dwarf the little houses even more. Matt pointed to one of the houses.

"That's the one. Do you want me to wait?"

Beth nodded and got out of the cruiser. Jody's house might have been nice once upon a time, but it sure wasn't very nice now. Beth felt a twinge of guilt. She had complained so much about Wheaton to Jody, but she lived in a nice house, in a nice neighborhood. She had no idea that Jody was so poor.

Beth knocked once. Then again. A woman answered the door. It took Beth a minute to realize that it was Lynette, Jody's mother. Dressed in a tattered housecoat and wearing no makeup, she looked a lot different from the last time Beth had seen her.

"Yes?" asked Lynette, staring vacantly at Beth.

Beth felt suddenly uneasy. "Hi."

Lynette made no response.

"I'm Beth, Jody's friend. We met yesterday." Still Lynette said nothing. It was as if she didn't remember ever laying eyes on Beth before.

"Is Jody here?"

Lynette shook her head in the negative.

"I was supposed to meet her," explained Beth.

"I told you she's not here," said Lynette firmly as she closed the door.

Beth couldn't believe it. Why was she so rude? And where in the heck was Jody? Beth walked past the cruiser and headed toward town on foot. She mumbled to herself unhappily.

"No luck, huh?" said Matt, driving next to her in the cruiser.

Beth just shook her head and kept walking.

"Jody isn't a bad kid," said Matt gently. "She's just not too dependable."

"You're telling me!" said Beth, practically shouting. She kicked up a cloud of dirt in frustration.

Matt reached over and opened the passenger door. "Come on, I'll take you home."

Beth got in. That Jody was unreliable seemed like a huge understatement to her.

A few moments later, Matt turned down a quiet street, heading toward town. He kept looking at Beth and then shaking his head.

"Boy, you sure look familiar," he said. "You're sure we haven't met?"

"I've never been here before," Beth replied. She

wasn't exactly in the mood for chatting.

"You and your mom bought Alice Young's old place, didn't you?" Matt persisted.

"My mother inherited it," replied Beth. "Alice was her aunt."

"Her aunt?" Matt said. Then something suddenly dawned on him. "Is your mother named Kate?!"

Beth nodded.

"Small town, small world," was all he would say.

When the cruiser reached Beth's new house, all she could see were her mother's feet, balancing precariously on the verandah ten feet up in the air. Beth looked up. Her mom was painting the upstairs window frames to match the front door.

Kate turned around. When she saw the sheriff's car her face went white. Beth and Matt got out, and Kate looked relieved but concerned.

"What happened?" she asked.

"Nothing," said Beth glumly. "Jody never showed. The sheriff gave me a ride home. I thought you were supposed to start working on your book today."

"I am," Kate insisted. "I'm thinking about it while I do some painting."

Matt smiled up at Kate. "The last time I saw you, our legs were tied together."

"Excuse me?" said Kate, looking at the sheriff with perplexed suspicion.

"Nice to see you again, *lambchop*." He turned to Beth. "That's what her aunt and uncle used to call her. She'd get so embarrassed." He turned back to Kate. "I'm Matt . . . Hollinger."

Kate's face lit up with recognition. "Matt! The three-legged race! We would have won, too—if you hadn't tripped! I'll be right down."

Kate climbed in through the window she had just painted, getting paint all over her hands. She looked at Matt sheepishly. Inside the phone rang.

When Kate went to answer the phone, Beth turned to Matt with a knowing grin. "You're hitting on my mother, aren't you?"

"Now wait a minute . . ." he said warningly, but his eyes and mouth registered amusement.

Kate appeared again at the upstairs window, holding up the receiver. "Beth, there's someone on the phone for you disguising her voice."

"Jody!" As if someone had electrocuted her with a power surge, Beth flew into the house and upstairs to her bedroom. Into the phone she said, "Mom, you can hang up now." She waited for the click, then, "Do you know how long I waited? Where were you?"

"What time do you have?" was all Jody said.

Beth looked at the clock. "9:47."

"At 9:57 look out your bedroom window and I will signal my location to you. Look for the flashing light.

51

Tell no one of my whereabouts." Jody hung up.

For ten of the longest minutes Beth could remember, she sat watching the clock. When the digital clock changed to 9:57, Beth looked out the window. Across the meadow from the edge of the woods came a sudden, glaring flash of light. The sun was reflecting on the glass, on and off, on and off. Jody was signaling with a compass. Beth took note of Jody's location, set the location in her mind's eye, then bounded down the stairs two at a time.

Kate and Matt were on the front porch with Grace from next door. The three of them were laughing hysterically when Beth shot past them, down the porch, and across the lawn. "Mom," she called out on the run, "I'm meeting Jody. I'll be back early—"

"Beth, wait!" Kate ran over to her daughter. "Where are the two of you off to?"

"You know, just around." Actually, Beth had no idea where exactly she was going.

"I don't want you getting in any trouble," said Kate, hesitating. "Mrs. Briggs says Jody has, well, some problems. She's rough . . . and she doesn't tell the—"

Beth interrupted her. "She just doesn't have any friends. Trust me, Mom."

Kate swallowed her doubts. "All right. But be home for dinner."

"I will. 'Bye, Mom!" called Beth as she ran out of

sight. Soon she was at the edge of the woods. The light began to flash again and Beth whispered, "Jody? Jody, are you there?" She was met with only silence. "Jody! Where are you?" she shouted.

Suddenly a hand covered her mouth as someone jumped her from behind. Beth felt herself being dragged backward and she stumbled to stay on her feet. Before she could begin to scream, the hand released her. It was Jody!

Beth was furious. She hated being scared like that. "What's the matter with you?"

"Why don't you just shout louder so they can hear my name in Canada?"

"Well, who cares who hears your name anywhere?" Beth retorted.

But Jody suddenly looked frightened. "Is anyone with you?"

"Of course not!" said Beth. "Jody, what's going on? Where were you this morning?"

"I was at the school."

"No you weren't," Beth insisted. "I waited there for you just like you said."

"I was inside, getting supplies." From within her backpack, Jody pulled out some junk food. Beth peered in. There were enough goodies to feed an army. Along with medical supplies. And an audiocassette player.

"How did you get all this?"

"I sure didn't pay for it," admitted Jody.

Beth was shocked. "You stole it?" Stealing was not good. Not good at all.

"Yeah. And when I saw you with the sheriff, I thought he was after me. I had to stay hidden."

"The sheriff didn't know you broke into the school. You're exaggerating again."

Again Jody looked scared. "Does he know where we're going? Does anybody know? You didn't tell anyone, did you?"

Beth was getting exasperated. "How could I tell when I don't even know?"

Jody looked relieved. With a dramatic flourish, she removed an old, weather-beaten book from her backpack. "Look at this, and you'll know!" Beth reached for the book, but Jody pulled it back.

"Careful, it's really old, it'll tear. It's from 1932."

Beth read the cover aloud. " 'Bear Mountain and the Legend of Molly Morgan.' "

Jody gingerly displayed the crumbling pages with their fading photographs and maps. "It's one of the books from the Historical Society."

"How did you get it?"

"One good thing about living in this place is that a lot of buildings close down, and when they do, you can find some great stuff," Jody smiled, happy at the memory of digging around Wheaton's old abandoned sites.

"It was bizarre, Beth. Like someone followed me there and made sure I found it." She pointed at a photo in the book. "That picture was taken over a hundred years ago. You know what's in that sack? Gold! And there's plenty more where that came from."

Beth was skeptical. "After a hundred years?"

"The mountain's still there, isn't it? My dad used to tell me the legend. Just like his father told him. But this book has secrets that nobody knows," Jody said. "Except me."

Beth indicated the cover of the book. "Who's Molly Morgan?"

"Only the greatest woman who ever lived!" Jody stated, returning the book to her backpack. "Come on. I'll tell you later." Jody set off briskly into the woods.

"How far is the mountain?" asked Beth.

"About fifteen miles."

"We can't walk that far."

"Who says we're walking?" Jody suddenly disappeared from view.

"Wait a minute!" Beth panicked. "Where are you?" Jody was nowhere to be seen. Ahead of Beth was only an unruly thicket of brush and brambles. "Jody?" Beth grew tense, spooked by the sudden quiet.

Out of nowhere came the bloodcurdling sound of an animal roar. Beth screamed and nearly tripped over herself trying to get out of there. The terrifying roar sounded again. Beth fell, scampering quickly to her feet. There in front of her was Jody, laughing her braying laugh and holding up the audiocassette player. Still chuckling, Jody clicked off the machine and out popped the cassette.

"Great sound effects, huh?"

Beth was suddenly more furious than she'd ever been. Being totally mysterious was one thing, and making her wait while she stole was pretty mean, not to mention wrong. But pulling a stunt like this just to humiliate her was totally unacceptable. Beth clenched her hands into fists and had to hold herself back from punching Jody smack in the nose.

"It was just a joke," said Jody, laughing.

"You're the joke!" yelled Beth. She whirled around, looking for a path that would lead her out of the woods and away from Jody. Jody's smile was suddenly gone. She knew that this time she'd gone too far.

"No wonder you have no friends," said Beth between clenched teeth, still circling for a path to get out. "No wonder you got left back. They should have put you all the way back—to nursery school!"

Jody recoiled, a devastated look on her face. Beth's words were like a kick in the stomach.

Beth stopped circling. "How do I get out of here?" she shouted. Beth turned to face Jody, and saw the look of hurt and betrayal on her new friend's face.

Jody pointed a direction through the woods. Beth headed that way, then hesitated, stopped, and quickly turned around.

Jody had already plowed ahead in a different direction through the brush.

Beth stood there, still angry at Jody, but now also angry at herself. "Jody, wait up!" she called, and clawed her way through to where Jody stood. They stared at each other for a moment, neither knowing what to say.

Jody finally broke the silence. "Who told you I was left back? I know, it was that brown-nose Tracy Briggs!" she said with her hands on her hips. "I don't want you thinking I'm dumb. I'm not dumb!"

"But I am for saying it," said Beth, suddenly very sorry indeed.

Jody resumed walking along the trail. "Well, are you coming to the mountain or not?"

Beth paused, then decided, catching up to Jody. "I really thought that was a bear. No more animal noises! Promise."

Jody chuckled. "I'm sorry if I scared you before."

"I wasn't that scared," Beth fibbed.

"Oh no?" taunted Jody. "Your eyeballs went *boiiiing!*" Jody laughed that hiccoughing guffaw of hers as if the mere thought of her prank was enough to send her into hysterics.

"You laugh like a horse," stated Beth.

"You look like one," Jody snapped back, starting off at a run and motioning for Beth to follow. Both girls raced around the mountain trail and came to a panting halt near a grassy slope. As they peered over the top, Beth gasped.

The view was incredible. The entire mountain seemed to open up, revealing a huge, copper-colored canyon curving through the mountains. Beth remembered the trip she had taken with her parents to the Grand Canyon three years before. This canyon was not as big, but somehow it seemed even grander.

"Here we are!" said Jody triumphantly, noting the impressed expression on Beth's face. "The Jody River. Well, it ought to be named after me. I'm the only one who ever comes here."

They ran down the hill to the river, where Jody didn't stop once she hit the knee-high water but kept heading around toward a cove obscured by trees. "Wait here!" she called out. "I have a surprise for you!"

"Jody, where are you? Are you goofing on me again?" Beth ran upriver where the trees ended, hoping to get a better look. Suddenly she heard the sound of a motor roaring to life.

"Get outta town!" Beth shouted over the noise. "That's your cassette again!"

But to Beth's total amazement, Jody sailed into view behind the wheel of an old but still functional motorboat. Captain Jody was wearing a naval officer's cap two sizes too large. "All aboard, me hearties!"

"Holy mo—" said Beth. The boat was painted in bright, mismatched colors like the Partridge Family bus. With a lawn chair, a lantern, a cowbell, a fog horn, and a shack that looked like it had been nailed together by Huckleberry Finn, this was no ordinary boat. Jody sounded the horn and Beth splashed her way toward the boat.

"This is incredible!" Beth said, climbing aboard. The boat set off down the river. "Where in the world did you get this?"

"There used to be a big paper mill near here. When it closed, a lot of boats got left behind. All this one really needed was a new motor. So I got one."

"You 'got' one?" Beth grinned. "OK, so tell me. Whose motor was it?"

"You accusing me of theft, Eastman?" said Jody playfully. "I paid twenty dollars for it."

"Where did you get the money?"

"I stole it from my mother's purse."

Beth laughed, despite the fact that she didn't particularly like or approve of this side of Jody. "Jody, you better watch yourself. Before you know it, you'll be robbing banks, and they'll throw you in jail for the rest of your life."

Jody's face registered total fear.

Beth noticed, but then the look was gone. Beth took a turn at the wheel while they traveled down the river, turning on the cassette player so Jody could dance on board. The greenery of the sloping meadow land gave way to the craggier, more foreboding cliff sides of the canyon. Jody took the wheel while Beth studied the ancient book about Molly Morgan and Bear Mountain.

Jody knew the whole book by heart and quoted excitedly. " 'It was 1849 and the rush was on. Farmers and teachers, millhands and preachers headed to California in search of gold.' Oregon was next, then it was our turn here in Washington. The biggest strike up here was at Bear Mountain."

Beth referred to the book. "Stop the party! Everybody go home! You only happened to leave out the most important thing: There's no gold left on Bear Mountain. Says so right here."

Jody took the book, turning the pages. "No, here, look at this. 'Whenever miners gather 'round campfires, they tell the tale of Bear Mountain's most famous prospector, a girl named Molly Morgan.' "

Jody went on to give Beth a rundown of Molly's story. Molly had been born in Scotland in 1900. She was exactly their age, twelve, when her father was killed in a factory explosion. Molly stole a loaf of bread to feed her family, and was arrested and sent to a workhouse where they worked people till they dropped.

But they couldn't keep her caged up, not Molly Morgan. Molly jumped from the workhouse window into the river below and swam for her life. They never caught her, thinking she drowned in the falls. Nothing could stop her. She stowed aboard a freighter and crossed the Atlantic to Canada. Then, by train, by foot, and by boat, she crossed the continent. She dreamed of getting rich. She dreamed of gold.

None of the miners wanted a girl with them. So Molly cut off her hair, smudged up her face, and the next thing anyone knew, a boy who called himself Morgan was one of the miners riding the boat to Bear Mountain. Molly Morgan had sailed down the same river that Beth and Jody were on!

During Molly's third time out on the mountain, the mine caved in. It was horrible, worse than an earthquake. Everything went dark. Gigantic rocks fell on top of the miners, crushing them all to death or suffocating them when the air supply dwindled. Nobody could have ever survived. Or so they said.

In 1931, just before the book came out, Jody explained, the police arrested a crazy mountain woman for making moonshine whiskey. The woman called herself Molly Morgan. All those years she had lived inside the mountain. And she told the police that if they would set her free, she would show them how to find a fortress of gold. She even offered to draw them a map. The officers simply thought she was crazy and threw her into jail. But they should have known they couldn't keep Molly Morgan locked up. Not for long.

She broke out of the jail house the same way she crashed out of the workhouse—she leaped out of the window. They chased her through the woods with dogs. But Molly made it safely to the river and grabbed a rowboat. The way the legend had been told, she went straight over the falls to her death. But they never found the body.

Jody paused in her story. "And you know why?" she asked Beth. "Because there wasn't any body to be found. You just know she survived and went right back to the mountain—"

"You're making this up," protested Beth. "You don't know any such thing. You can't even be sure she was the real Molly. Anyone can pretend to be Molly."

"No, Beth. It's her," said Jody, in a hushed voice. "It's got to be. Sometimes when I'm out in the woods, I can *feel* her. I can feel her watching!"

Jody looked down from one bank of the river to the other, as if Molly could be watching right that very minute.

Spooked, Beth did the same thing. "Look what she's got me doing!" she said to herself and then to Jody. "I've got more gold in my teeth than there is in that mountain. Even if that crazy woman was telling the truth, don't you think someone would have found the gold by now?"

"That's just it!" said Jody, exasperated. "No one ever looked because they thought she was crazy. But what if that mountain woman really was the elusive Molly Morgan?"

Jody steered the boat through a narrowing stretch of water nestled between the steep stone mountains. "And what if there really is a fortress of gold? What if it's waiting for us right there—right there in Bear Mountain?"

Jody gestured down river. Beth's mouth dropped open. Half a mile away, shrouded in the shade of the trees, stood Bear Mountain. It was covered with dozens and dozens of caves, both natural and human made.

"This is *my* river," said Jody. "And that is *my* mountain. I started coming six months ago, as soon as I read the book. And now it's finally here. June 21st."

"Where do all those caves go?"

"Some are mine shafts. And one of them leads to the fortress of gold." There was no doubt in Jody's voice that she was right.

"But which one? There are so many?" Beth asked.

Jody checked her watch. "Looks like we'll find out in . . . twelve minutes."

She shut off the motor. The boat slowly drifted with the current. "In the book, Molly Morgan says you can find the cave at high noon the day of the summer solstice, the longest day of the year. That was the only time when the sun's rays were at the exact right angle to shine into the cave and bounce back. We'll see the reflection from here. Molly said it was so bright she nearly went blind."

The two girls stared at the mountain as if it were an old Egyptian sphinx, about to reveal all of its ancient secrets.

Beth was quiet. At first, Jody's dreams of endless riches had seemed so crazy. But as the story of Molly Morgan began to seep into Beth's imagination, the more real it all seemed. And now, as they got closer and closer to the secret cave, Beth found herself wishing with all her might that the treasure was there. Jody just had to be right.

Beth turned to look at her friend, who was totally absorbed in the mountain scenery. Staring at Jody's intense expression, Beth realized that she was in for the long haul. If Jody believed with all her heart that her dreams were real, so would Beth. She studied the mountain. She was filled with anticipation. They just had to find that cave. They just had to!

Chapter 7

The girls waited on the boat for Molly Morgan's prophecy to come true.

"As soon as I get my hands on that gold, I'm outta here!" proclaimed Jody. "I'm taking a gondola down the Grand Canal and a camel across the Sahara Desert. I'm going surfing on the Black Sea and skinny dipping in the Gulf of Mexico. And then I'm going up—to outer space!"

"You're already there," quipped Beth. Jody was fun, but crazy. There may be a treasure up there, but no one found real gold these days. No one.

Jody checked her watch again. "Eleven fifty-one. Nine more minutes. She looked up. The sun burned in the center of a bright blue sky, but beginning to drift in from the west were ominous gray clouds. Rain clouds.

"You better hope those clouds don't get in your way," said Beth.

The dark clouds moved closer to the sun, but did not block the sun's rays yet. Beth and Jody were suddenly apprehensive as they looked from the clouds to their watches. It was a race against time.

"Ten, nine, eight . . ." they chanted, looking up as the clouds spread like an ink stain onto the edge of the bright sun.

"Seven, six, five, four, three, two, one!" The sun's rays swept up onto the mountain. Part of the way up the half-mile-high eastern slope, as if a spotlight had been switched on, a cave with a diamond-shaped entrance glowed with golden luminescence! The entire world seemed to light up. Even Jody's and Beth's faces were lit up by the nearly blinding glow.

"That's it!" cried Jody. "Start counting the money! It's real! It's all ours. Watch out, world. Here I come!" Jody rang the cowbell and blew the foghorn full-blast. It was so noisy that the frogs napping on the lily pads dived for cover. Flocks of birds in overhanging branches scattered in the sky. Deer in the nearby woods ran for their lives.

Beth stared in disbelief at the glowing cave.

"Well, say something!" Jody demanded. "You're too shocked, right?"

Beth was flustered. "It could be an illusion, Jody. The sun could be bouncing off some rocks—"

"Yeah, the rocks in your head!" said Jody. "Why can't you believe what's right in front of your eyes?"

"There's only one way to find out, and we're not

going to," answered Beth.

"Why not?"

"You can't expect us to climb up there."

Jody ignored her and started the motor. The boat began to speed through the water.

"We can't, Jody," protested Beth. "I promised my mother I'd be home early."

Jody shot her a look as if she had totally lost it. "You mean if you were on the boat with Christopher Columbus just when he spotted land, you'd honestly tell him to turn around because your mother wanted you home early?"

"OK, OK, don't get hysterical, I hear you. But climbing that mountain is still too dangerous."

"No it isn't," Jody promised. "Just trust me."

"That's what I told my mother," Beth mumbled to herself. Before she could think of anything else to say, they sailed through the entrance to a mammoth cave. They were inside the mountain!

Jody cut the power and the boat drifted across a lagoon. "Hello . . . hello . . ." shouted Jody.

And back the echo came, "Helllllooooo."

"My name is Beth."

"Beth-eth-eth-eth."

"Good," pronounced Jody, "now the bats know we're here!"

"Bats? Oh my God!" Beth panicked, grabbing the

first thing she saw on the deck, an old blanket, and diving under it.

"Relax," said Jody. "I was only kidding."

Beth slowly emerged from the safety of the blanket. "Where are you taking us?"

"My condo."

"Your what?" Beth peered ahead of her as Jody steered under a canopy of stalactites. Nervous, and more than a little frightened, Beth reverted back to her old cautious self. "Jody, I want to know where we're going! It looks like it's easy to get lost in here."

Jody did not reply. She was concentrating on something ahead of her. Beth looked but couldn't make out anything but more cave walls and more eerie darkness.

Just as the boat passed beneath the overhanging stone spires, Jody leaped up and grabbed onto a spire. She chinned herself off the deck of the boat and hung there. "So long, Beth. Hope you're a good sailor."

Terrified, Beth yelled, "Get down from there!"

"OK, if you insist . . ." Jody said mischievously. She waited for the boat to move past—and dropped into the water!

Beth raced to the side, looking over the edge for her friend. Jody popped up to the surface of the water.

"Say you'll climb the mountain—" Jody said, a laughing warning in her voice.

Beth looked ahead. The boat was about to crash

into a stone wall. Beth grabbed the wheel and steered sharply in the other direction, but she accidentally hit the throttle and the boat picked up speed, heading straight toward the opposite wall.

"Beth, wait! You're going to crash!" Jody yelled from the water.

Beth quickly readjusted the throttle and the engine finally slowed down. She regained control and straightened the boat. Her nerves were shot, and the adrenaline slowed down its fast course through her bloodstream.

"What do I do now?" Beth asked. There was no response. "Jody? Where are you? Don't play any more of your stupid games!" A curve in the water's path forced her to negotiate a tight turn. She did it without a hitch, missing the cave walls by at least a foot on both sides of the boat.

Around the curve the cave opened into a circular pool under a domed ceiling. And there was Jody, balanced on a ridge on the cave's wall—and standing on her head. "Hey! How come you're upside-down?" Jody laughed her horsy laugh.

Beth sighed, cutting the motor. Would her friend ever get normal?

Jody finished securing the boat, tying it to a stone post near the ridge where she had stood on her hands moments before. Beth waited for her on the ridge, the backpack over her shoulder.

"Let's go, follow me," said Jody.

"Where?" Beth needed more information this time. There were too many surprises during the last few hours, and Beth never knew what to expect.

"I told you," replied Jody. "My condo." Jody grabbed the backpack and pulled out a flashlight.

The going was slow. Jody lead them first through a portal in the cave wall. They climbed up a passageway so dark that the beam of the flashlight seemed to cut a tube in the darkness in front of them. Then up a stone stairway they walked, careful not to slip on the slick surface kept wet by a steady stream of water coming from various cracks in the walls.

"Wipe your shoes," ordered Jody, indicating a welcome mat at their feet.

Beth laughed and did as her hostess demanded. Jody wiped her shoes and stepped down through another portal, moving aside for Beth to see.

"The condo!" Jody said with pride in her voice.

Beth could not believe what she was seeing. The awesome stone chamber was the ultimate in home decorating. Different pieces of mismatched carpet covered the floor from cave wall to cave wall. Various pieces of standing stone were also upholstered in multicolored carpet pieces, creating comfortable furniture. It was the perfect place to hide from adults.

The floor of Jody's condo was actually the top tier of a series of cave terraces, like a stone wedding cake, that descended into a canal some thirty feet below. Light from outside seeped into the chamber from the entrance to the canal.

"Please," said Jody, "do come into the sitting room, won't you?"

The sitting room featured a chair and a sofa. Beth lifted the tattered yet comfortable upholstery to reveal more zany rock formations!

"It looks like real furniture," Beth said, laughing.

"They're antiques," said Jody, mocking a hoity-toity British accent. "Been in the family for years. Four trillion years."

Jody gestured to a table—another stone formation covered with a ragged tablecloth. Atop the table was a jug that caught the water trickling down from an overhanging spire.

"This is amazing!" Beth said. She was impressed, yet again. "*You* are amazing!"

"Running water. Free rent. What more could I want?" Jody said. She was obviously very happy that Beth liked her secret hideaway.

"A TV," answered Beth facetiously.

Jody reached behind a corner of a stone, and *voilá*! She pulled out a small, battery operated pocket television. Beth looked at it, then spied a metal identification tag on the back.

" 'Property of Wheaton Elementary School.' Oh, Jody," she said, sounding disappointed. She gave Jody a look of disapproval.

Jody evaded Beth's face, turning toward a recess in the cave wall with clothes hanging from stone "hooks."

As Jody slowly pulled off her sopping clothes and changed into another pair of cutoff jeans, Beth said, "Does your mother know you come here?"

"My mother?" Jody exclaimed. "My mother probably thinks I'm still in the next room. You've heard about her, haven't you?" Jody faced Beth, wanting to know what else she knew about Jody's personal life.

"Heard what?" Beth said.

"You're a bad liar, Beth," said Jody. "Your whole face twitches."

Beth didn't know what to say. She sure wasn't going to say, I heard your mom is a boozer, to a girl who was rapidly becoming the best friend she'd ever had in the whole wide world. "I heard . . ." Beth faltered, "that she's . . . not well . . ."

"Not well?" Jody laughed ruefully. "Every door you open in our house, bottles come rolling out. It smells like a brewery." Jody snapped her jeans shut.

Jody's admission stunned Beth. So it was true! Jody's mom was an alcoholic. Everything Beth knew about alcoholics was bad. They drank first thing in the morning. Their personalities could change from charming to abusive in a split second. Alcoholics had a hard time holding down steady jobs and relationships were often disastrous with family members as well as other people. And under it all, Beth guessed, alcoholics were probably all very sad people who thought they had something to hide—or hide from.

"What about Ray?" Beth said gently. She didn't want to show how sorry she felt for Jody.

"Ray? He's even worse," said Jody. "That's why she likes him so much. The two of them can get plastered together all the time."

Beth felt terrible for her friend. What was it like living in a family like that? She watched Jody take off her wet shirt and twist it in a tube to squeeze the rest of the water out.

Beth could barely contain her gasp. A gauze bandage completely covered Jody's left shoulder. Purple and yellow bruises showed from outside the strips of surgical tape that had been criss-crossed over the bandage, making it look like Jody, wrapping it herself, had had a hard time reaching the tape onto her back. It was obviously a nasty wound. So that's what it's like living in her house, Beth thought to herself as Jody pulled on a new shirt.

"Oh, Jody," Beth said aloud, "what happened to you?" She suddenly felt completely sick to her stomach.

Chapter 8

Jody, pulling the hem of the shirt down over her waist, was startled. She had obviously forgotten about the bandage she wore.

"Uh, it's from when you almost killed me with your bicycle," she said quickly. "Don't worry, I'm not going to sue you."

Beth thought a moment. "That was your right shoulder. And that was also over a week ago. What happened?"

"Don't worry about me," said Jody, sounding like she was trying to be brave but didn't feel brave. "I'm pretty tough. I know how to take care of myself."

"What are you talking about?"

Jody paused, then threw her whole body into the story as she began to reenact it. "Well, Ray and my mother got smashed. He treats her pretty bad when he gets like that. She used to fight back, but she doesn't anymore. He's worse now 'cause he's out of work. This monster comes out of him—and that's when I get out!"

Beth stared, transfixed, her mind racing. This couldn't be true, could it? Jody's mother was also getting beaten up? How could a grown-up live like that? They weren't even married. And even if they were, no one had the right to treat another person like that, no matter how much of an alcoholic they were.

Jody took a breath and continued. "I just leave, to the woods, to my condo, anywhere to get away from that sound. Those awful sounds. But last night there was something new—there was no sound. I was just so scared for her. I knew I had to help her. I *had* to help her." Jody stopped, obviously upset by the memory of the previous night.

Beth wondered if that was why Jody's mom was so weird at the door that morning. "What did you do?" she asked her friend.

"I was scared, but I went back. My mama was on the floor and he was coming at her. I thought this time he was going to kill her! I grabbed my fishing pole and flew through the air to protect her. Everything was a blur. I felt the pole go into him like a spear, and then it snapped, broken. He threw me and I hit my shoulder against something sharp, the corner of the table or something. I got up and ran like hell into the woods. I heard him running after me, screaming. And then I couldn't hear him anymore. I saw him fall. I knew he was dead."

"Dead?! Was there blood?"

Jody nodded.

"You're sure he was dead?" Beth asked.

"He wasn't moving. He wasn't breathing. I walked around him three times. I called his name. I leaned over him. Trust me. Worm food."

"You mean there's a dead body just laying there in the woods?"

Jody nodded. "Until someone finds him."

"What about your mother? She saw the whole thing!" Beth couldn't believe this mess. A real murder? An actual dead body? Poor Jody must have been so frightened from it all.

"She was out cold. I told you," Jody said softly. She sat down on her carpeted rock sofa, slumping over to put on different socks and sneakers.

Beth sat down beside her. "We'll talk to my mother. She'll know what to do—"

"No!" Jody cried. "Beth, swear! Swear you won't say anything."

"But you need help!" Beth said forcefully. "You need help." Beth leaped to her feet. "This is ridiculous! Come back with me and tell them the truth! It was all in self-defense. Tell them how Ray was beating your mother."

Jody shook her head. "They would only take Ray's side. They're going to say he was trying to straighten me out so I killed him."

Beth could tell that Jody had already thought about getting help and had quickly dismissed the idea. "But they'd never say that!" Beth argued.

"Oh no?" challenged Jody. "You liked him, too. Everybody likes him. But they don't feel that way about me. They'd never, *ever* believe me. Look at all that stuff Tracy and Samantha told you. And you'll hear it from your mother, too. Just wait."

Beth was startled. She had heard it from her mother already.

"They always said I'd end up in prison. Well, sorry folks, I'll have to disappoint you. I'm staying right here, just the way Molly Morgan did. Free!" Jody rose and looked out across the expanse of the chamber, lost in her dream.

Beth suddenly knew why Jody was so adamant about the existence of Molly Morgan and her fortress of gold. Jody had to believe in it. It was all she had.

As if reading her mind, Jody said, "Molly Morgan had a hard life, too. But she never cried. She escaped from the workhouse and came to the mountain. She might have stood right here." Jody walked to the edge of the cliff, overlooking the canal.

"She did not die in that cave-in," insisted Jody, addressing the water more than Beth. "That mountain woman was Molly Morgan. She lived inside these walls and she found that fortress of gold. And I'll find it, too!" She turned to Beth. "You can steer the boat yourself, can't you?"

Beth was surprised. What was Jody getting at? "I think so. Why?"

"I was hoping you could bring me food if I run out. Or just visit, so I could have someone to talk to. I may have to stay here a long time, at least until I figure out my next move."

Beth was touched. Of course she'd help Jody. She'd do anything to make it better for her, to help her get out of her terrible trouble. "You know I'll help you," she promised.

"Good!" said Jody, trying to brighten up. "That's the second promise you made today. . . ."

"What's the first?"

"To climb up to the cave," stated Jody in a matter-of-fact tone. "You said—"

"Forget it! No! No way."

"It's not like we have to climb up the side of the mountain," said Jody. "We take the passageways the miners used. They wind all the way up inside the mountain and let us out right by the cave with the gold. We go right through there." Jody pointed across the chamber to another portal, accessible by a ridge that circled all the way around the wall to the other side of the chamber.

"Here, look." Jody rummaged in the backpack and found the old book. She opened it to one of the maps.

Beth came closer to look.

"This is a map of that passageway," Jody explained. "No one has laid eyes on this for years. See, the passageway looks like a spider web, it leads to lots of different caves."

Beth watched as Jody traced a route with her finger.

"And now we know the cave we want to go to. This is the way to get there!"

"No!" Beth stood up. Her legs suddenly ached from crouching. "I never drove a boat by myself, all alone. I've got to give myself plenty of time to get home while there's still daylight."

Jody looked at her friend and nodded in understanding, then said, "You're not going to tell them where I am, are you?"

"I told you I wouldn't!" Beth said. Why didn't Jody trust *her* of all people? Beth didn't lie to her. But Jody was used to people turning on her, Beth guessed, maybe that was why. She took the flashlight from Jody and started out of the condo.

Jody followed her. "Are you mad at me?" Jody asked, her voice full of anxiety and fear.

Beth shook her head in the negative.

"You are, I can tell," said Jody, sounding disappointed and hopeless.

Beth whirled around. "I'm just angry that this happened to you!"

Beth and Jody both burst into tears at the same time, hugging each other. "You didn't do anything wrong!" Beth said through her tears. "You shouldn't have to hide."

"I never meant to kill him," Jody said woefully.

"I'll come back to see you every single week of the summer. Cross my heart," said Beth. She grabbed Jody's hand as they went down the stone staircase toward the secured boat.

Suddenly an ear-splitting thunderclap roared through the cave. "Don't be frightened," said Jody, "it's just a little rain. The echoes make it sound much worse than it really is."

The cave pool lay before them in a turmoil of waves and thunder. "A little rain?" asked Beth, as if Jody must be kidding. This wasn't a little rain, this was a storm. She watched as the wind whipped up the water in the cave pool. "Jody, look! The boat!"

Around the ridge, the boat had gotten loose from its mooring. Beth and Jody raced to the prow. Beth reached the mooring rope first and grabbed onto it, but with the next swoop of wind, the boat lurched and she was yanked into the churning waters.

Jody watched as Beth pulled on the rope and managed to hoist herself aboard the bouncing boat. She staggered to the motor and started it, but lashed by wind and rain, she gave it too much gas. Beth was knocked off her feet as the boat shot forward.

Jody raced around the ridge toward her, yelling, "Grab the wheel!"

The boat spun like a top and then shot into the cavern entrance. Beth was heading straight toward a wall. The boat was totally out of control.

"Beth, watch out!" screamed Jody desperately.

Beth finally grabbed the wheel. But it was too late. The boat raced into a narrow embankment and crashed into a cave wall. The sound of splintered wood mixed with the roar of falling stone. The impact unleashed a rock slide of large stone slabs falling loose from the cave ceiling.

Jody leaped off the ridge onto the embankment and reached Beth. Her friend was sprawled on her back on the floor of the shattered boat, her right leg pinned under the pile of stone slabs.

"Get these off me. My leg's stuck," said Beth, near tears and wincing from the pain. "My arm, I can't move it. It really hurts."

A gust of wind blew sheets of rain into the cave as Jody tried desperately to move the slabs. She pushed all her weight against the immense stones, but they wouldn't budge an inch.

"I can't do it!" Jody cried, her voice echoing in the

cave. "It's like trying to move the whole mountain!"

"You need to get help. I'll just have to lay here," said Beth, feeling weak.

"You can't just lay there! The tide!" said Jody, a fraction of a second later regretting saying it.

Beth noticed Jody's panicked expression. "What about the tide? How much time do we have before I could . . . drown?" Beth raised her head to look around her. The storm was tossing up sheets of water onto the embankment and it looked like the water was rising pretty steadily.

"You're not going to drown! We have till sometime after dark. It's the longest day of the year," Jody paused to calculate. "We have about eight or nine hours or so, maybe more."

"How close are we to civilization?"

Jody brightened. "There's a highway west of here, on the other side of the forest."

"How far?" said Beth, wincing again from the pain shooting into her arm.

"I'm not sure, but I know I could reach it way before dark. Four or five hours, tops, not even that if the rain stops!"

Beth looked at her and reached over with her free arm to squeeze Jody's hand. She looked up into her friend's face, but didn't speak.

Jody squeezed back and gave Beth a quick, reassuring smile. She looked outside the cave into the stormy darkness. She'd have to hurry. Both girls knew that if the rain didn't let up Beth wouldn't have much chance of surviving.

Chapter 9

Back at the house, Kate was holed up in the kitchen. Working at the kitchen table, she scribbled on a large pad. Sketches for her book were scattered across the table. With all this rain, she had no choice but to finally work on her story about the lostrich.

She raised her head and stared out the window again. A momentary ray of sunlight shot through the dark, cloudy sky. It looked like the rain just might let up. Kate opened the window a crack for a breath of fresh air.

The front lawn was covered with an inch of fresh water from the summer storm. Beth's bicycle lay on its side near the front porch. Where were those girls, anyway? Kate wondered. She hoped they were nowhere near the creek, which would be swollen by now into flowing rapids.

She reluctantly picked up her pencil and resumed sketching, but she couldn't shake off a feeling of foreboding. They shouldn't be out in this weather. If Beth didn't get her butt home soon, Kate swore she'd ground her for a week.

Back at the boat wreck, Jody left Beth's side for a moment to run up to the condo for the backpack. By the time she returned, the deluge had subsided and the sun was peeking out of the clouds, lighting up the cave entrance.

"The rain's stopping!" said Beth.

"I know! That's good!" Jody said, grabbing cookies, the radio, and TV from the backpack. "Food, fun, you name it, we've got it."

"How about a bulldozer?" Beth said ruefully.

Jody removed a blanket from the backpack and spread it over Beth. She had slipped into take-charge mode, and was speaking now with confidence and authority. "Don't worry about a thing, I've got a great plan. As soon as I reach the highway, I'll stop the first car I see, and I'll have them call the cops. I'll ride with them to the phone to make sure nothing goes wrong with the call. Then I'll skedaddle. I have it all set in my mind."

Jody propped the backpack under Beth's head and continued, "I can't talk to the cops myself or let them find me. They'd arrest me. I'll have to disappear."

"Where will you go?" Beth asked.

"Nobody knows the woods like I do. My dad taught

me good. I'll hang out in the woods for awhile, till it's safe to come back to my condo." She paused. "We need something for you to say when you're rescued. Tell them we went boating and got lost. Nothing about Ray. And nothing about the gold!" Jody clasped Beth's hand. "I'll come through for you. I swear to you, you can count on me. Be strong. Like Molly. Say it, strong like Molly."

"Strong, like Molly," repeated Beth.

Jody checked her compass. Then she abruptly turned and waded into the cave waters, swimming toward the entrance. She raised her head above the water and shouted back to Beth, "I'll do it, city girl!"

Beth watched, filled with mixed emotions of fear for herself, anticipation of her rescue, and love for her friend. Jody splashed out of the cave and began swimming up the river. Jody never heard Beth say between trembling lips, "I know you will!"

Jody swam out into the river under the clearing skies. To her sides were the tall canyon cliff sides, impossible to scale. The water was her only avenue out.

At first she swam as fast as she could, but her arms began to tire so she had to slow her pace. After a while, she raised her head from the water and dog paddled to get her bearings. Elation and relief coursed through her aching muscles when she saw the meadow lands just around the next bend in the river.

Jody swam toward the shore, where the cliff sides gave way to green meadows, collapsing on her back on the bank. She looked up at the sky, the sun giving her a surge of will, leaped to her feet, and continued trekking across the meadow toward the forest, soon disappearing into the immense spread of evergreens.

After the rain, the forest glistened with greens and golds lit up by darting shafts of sun. It looked magical, as if fairies, trolls, and leprechauns were waiting just around the next tree trunk. Jody checked her compass frequently, making her own path among the trees as she walked for hours.

Gazing up at the sky from a break in the trees, Jody squinted. The sun, streaked across the sky, was beginning its descent. Darkness was not far away.

"Just be strong, Beth," Jody said aloud to herself as she picked up her pace. "I'll make it. I won't let you down. Be strong, like Molly."

Inside the chilly cave, Beth was shivering. It was cold despite the blanket wrapped over her, and she had never felt so alone in her life. She tried to move her leg, but could not.

Turning her head toward the embankment, she noted that the water level had risen another foot or so. She could feel the water creeping up her back toward her neck. Beth closed her eyes and started to recite poems in her mind.

Jody was running through the woodland, gathering speed to help her up the steep grade of the next leg of her journey. She struggled up the hillside strewn with boulders, rocks sliding past her as her hands and feet unearthed them. She slid back, losing ground, but dug in her heels and climbed back up, finally pulling herself onto the peak.

Breathing loudly from the effort of the climb, she sat for a moment to rest. The late afternoon sun had almost hit the horizon. It wouldn't be long before dark.

Ignoring her weariness, Jody rose—and froze. She held her breath, not even blinking. There, staring her in the face, was a bear!

The bear stood on its hind legs and roared at Jody, its huge teeth bared menacingly. Jody froze from fear and held her breath, not moving a muscle.

Beth had run out of Pooh poems. The water had now reached her neck and the sunlight was almost gone. She thought about turning on the radio, but felt too tired to move. She was so cold, so very cold.

"Be strong, like Molly," she croaked. Her voice was too weak. The cave echoed back silence in response.

• • •

Eventually, the bear must have decided that Jody wasn't meaty enough for a substantial feast, for it stopped roaring, gave a parting sniff in her direction, and abruptly turned around. It lowered itself and started to wander off. As soon as it was out of sight, Jody began to breathe normally again. And she was off and running.

She emerged from the forest on the side of a hill. The sun was just a dot on the horizon, a glowing ball of yellow and orange. She sprinted down the hill toward a grove of trees.

Having rested during her encounter with the bear, Jody bolted through the trees like a human blur. She stumbled over thick undergrowth and fell. The wind was knocked out of her, preventing her from standing so she crawled for a few feet to catch her breath. Suddenly her hand slapped pavement. At that moment, the glowing ball of the sun melted into the earth. Nighttime had officially begun.

Jody got to her feet and peered down the asphalt ribbon that was the county road. There was a spot coming toward her. The spot grew larger and larger until she saw that it was a police car.

Jolted, Jody started back into the trees, crouching low as the car slowly began to pass. She couldn't stop this car, they would surely arrest her! But then Jody thought of Beth—what if another car didn't pass for a long time? She ran out of the woods to the roadside and began shouting frantically and waving her arms.

From his rearview mirror, Sergeant Weller saw someone moving in the road. He slowed down again. So he had seen something after all!

He put the car into reverse and backed up to what looked like a young girl. A filthy young girl with tree leaves in her hair, covered from head to toe with dried mud. Lit up by the flashing lights of the police cruiser, she looked more like a wood sprite than a human.

He got out of the car and walked toward her, squinting a little. "What are you doing way out here?"

He watched her eyes when she didn't respond. She looked terrified. Her eyes traveled from his officer's nightstick at his side, to the glint of his badge, to the gun in his holster, looking like she was about to bolt. She stared at him, her eyes again focusing in on the nightstick, staring, staring, staring. Then her eyes rolled back in her head and she passed out, collapsing in a heap on the pavement.

Jody woke up to a strong dose of smelling salts being waved back and forth under her nose. Sergeant Weller was leaning over her at the roadside.

"I won't let her down, I won't," she said in a daze.

"How are you feeling?" asked the sergeant.

Jody took a moment to get her bearings, then as Weller helped her sit up, she said quickly, "My friend, my friend, please help my friend. She's trapped under a rock slide at Bear Mountain! You've got to help her!"

Weller's face registered surprise. "You walked all the way here from Bear Mountain? My goodness!" He walked over to his car, keeping an eye on Jody to make sure she didn't faint again. "Where on the mountain is she?"

"The entrance," Jody began to explain, watching as Weller reached into his car and spoke over the police radio.

After a few moments he addressed her again. "What's your friend's name?"

"Beth Eastman."

"She your age?" he asked.

"Yes."

"Where's she from?"

"Wheaton," replied Jody as Weller repeated the information into the radio and continued talking to the authorities.

Jody's mission was accomplished. Beth was going to be rescued, just as Jody had promised. While Weller's attention was directed at his radio, Jody, still sitting on the ground, began to inch backward toward the trees to make her getaway.

Weller turned to her abruptly. "And you are—?"

Jody was startled and stopped moving. "What?"

"What's your name, Miss?" The sergeant looked at her expectantly.

"My name?" repeated Jody, stalling for time. "Molly. Molly Morgan."

Beth spit out the water that was now lapping up across her chin and into her mouth. She stirred, trying to keep her head up out of the water. A faint sound from somewhere far off made her keep still. Could it be? Then the sound built into the unmistakable whirring of a helicopter.

"Down here!" screamed Beth. "I'm down here! You did it, Jody! You did it!"

The State Police Rescue Squad helicopter hovered above the entrance to Bear Mountain. Floodlights illuminated the scene. Beth could hear the rescue workers shouting to one another above the chopper's deafening blades as they lowered equipment to other workers on a raft below.

Hank, the Squad Leader, rushed to Beth's side. He smiled down at Beth reassuringly. "Well," he shouted to be heard above the noise, "this looks like a nice, quiet spot. Would you mind if we liven things up and make a little noise?"

Beth shook her head. No, she wouldn't mind at all. Hank and another person placed protective gear over

Beth's face and upper body. Moments later, a loud drill burrowed through the stone slab atop Beth's leg. Through his protective gear, Beth could barely see the worker's face concentrating on cutting the stone away without injuring Beth any further. Soon, the slabs broke apart and splintered into a shower of rocks. Beth's leg was freed!

"Let me see you move your leg," said Hank to Beth. He held her leg gently as she raised and lowered it.

"Nothing seems to be broken," he said as Beth sighed. "Let's get you home."

Chapter 10

Kate waited at her front door, arms wrapped around her body as Matt's squad car pulled up to the house.

He got out of the car and quickly went to her. He gently took one of her arms, but she broke out into a run and jumped into the still running squad car. The doors slammed shut and the cruiser sped away, siren and lights whirring into the night.

Jody got off the table of the examining room and slipped on her shirt over her bandaged shoulder as the paramedic finished examining her. Through the open door, Jody could see Sergeant Weller at his desk in the squad room.

Weller's phone rang. He picked it up and asked the caller to hang on when the medic brought Jody in.

"So how's our Molly?" he asked the paramedic.

"That's a mean-looking bruise she's got on her shoulder," the paramedic answered, throwing the sergeant a significant look. "They'll have a better look at her over at the hospital."

"I'll do the honors," said Weller. "Thanks, Mike."

The paramedic turned to Jody. " 'Bye now, Molly. Great going!" He tousled her hair. "They're gonna give you a medal for saving your friend's life." He left with a wave, smiling.

Jody looked surprised but proud as she watched him go. Weller led her to an empty desk, where a burger, fries, and a soda were waiting.

"I'll bet you're starving," he said. "This ought to hold you till we get you home."

Jody tensed up but took the seat she was offered. Weller returned to his desk. "By the way, your friend's going to be fine."

Jody sighed with relief and Weller turned back to the phone call. "Sorry for the interruption, Matt," he said into the receiver.

Jody heard the name. What was Wheaton's sheriff, Matt Hollinger, going to tell Sergeant Weller? That she killed Ray?

Weller spoke into the phone. "The paramedics just had a look at Molly. She's OK," he paused. "You know, Molly. The girl here. Molly." Weller looked puzzled as he listened on the phone. He suddenly turned and stared sharply at Jody.

Jody turned away, frightened, looking through an open door that led outside. The front door of the squad room was also open, and Jody could see right out to the road in front. She was wondering whether the time to make her escape was right now, when the sergeant's attention was diverted to his phone call.

Weller said into the phone, "Yeah, I think I get the picture. OK, I'll take care of it." Weller hung up. He looked probingly at Jody's back, then approached her.

Jody sensed the sergeant's presence behind her. She turned around in her chair and put her arms straight out in front of her like a robot.

"What's that for?" asked Weller.

"Handcuffs," Jody said simply.

Weller chuckled to himself.

Jody, completely thrown by Weller's mild reaction, lowered her arms. "You're not going to arrest me?"

"Not unless you've done something a little more serious than giving me a phony name," he replied.

Jody was silent. Had they not yet found Ray's body? Should she confess? Escape?

The rescue helicopter carrying Beth landed in the field next to Wheaton's high school. Beth was taken off on a stretcher by Hank and the rescue worker who had cut the stone slabs off her. Medical technicians took over, carrying the stretcher toward a waiting ambulance. As the distance between them opened up, Beth called out a goodbye and Hank waved in return.

Kate and Matt ran toward the stretcher, Kate breaking away from Matt and rushing over to Beth with outstretched arms.

Beth lifted her head up more from the stretcher. "Mom!" Before she could say boo, her mother was all over her.

"Oh, Beth. Oh, Beth. Oh my—are you all right?" Kate didn't wait for an answer but smothered her daughter with kisses.

Across the field, Matt and Hank were conferring. Matt looked up at Beth briefly as Hank handed him Jody's backpack. From inside he pulled out the school's portable TV, their audiocassette player, and the old book and maps of Bear Mountain.

Kate still hovered over Beth, hugging her daughter as the medics walked Beth over toward the ambulance. "They said your arm is sprained," Kate said, choking back sobs. "And there's something with your knee, we don't know yet."

One of the medics gently ushered Kate to the side so they could move the stretcher into the back of the ambulance.

"I'm really OK," Beth said to one of the medics. "Can't I just go home?"

Matt arrived and helped the medics push the stretcher into the ambulance. "Not until the doctors look the two of you over."

"The two of us?" Beth asked, startled.

"You and Jody," Matt answered.

"Jo—?" began Beth. But the ambulance doors were closed. She heard a door slam and the siren began to wail. The ambulance drove off into the night.

Once at the county hospital, Beth was placed on a stretcher with Kate and Matt walking quickly by her side. A nurse whisked the stretcher away from the ambulance toward the hospital entrance just as Sergeant Weller's highway patrol car pulled in.

As the car drove slowly by, Beth saw Jody through the windshield. "Jody!" Beth yelled, bolting off of her stretcher before anyone could stop her.

Jody jumped out of the police cruiser before it stopped and called out, "Beth!" The two girls quickly ran toward each other across the parking oval, Beth limping.

Kate lurched forward. "No, Beth—"

But Matt gently held her back. "Let her go."

Jody grabbed Beth just as she was about to lose her balance. They embraced.

"I never thought I'd see you again!" Beth cried.

"They didn't get anything out of you, did they?" whispered Jody anxiously.

"No—" began Beth, but Jody interrupted her.

"Got to make this fast," Jody said. "They don't

know about Ray, nobody said a thing, guess they didn't find the body yet. I've got to disappear." Beth opened her mouth to object, but Jody continued. "Remember our plan. Keep your mouth shut."

"Got it!" Beth agreed.

"I've got to make a break for it. When the time's right, I'll head back to the condo."

Beth reached out and hugged Jody again, but the nurse arrived and eased Beth back onto the stretcher.

Kate was very upset. "What's the matter with you, Beth?" she said, and immediately led Beth away as Sergeant Weller took Jody by the hand.

A pickup truck screeched into the parking round. Almost before it stopped, Lynette Salerno jumped out, yelling, "Jody!" She rushed to her daughter, her eyes brimming with tears. Lynette gently placed her hands on Jody's arms. "Oh, Jody, baby. What now?" She pulled her daughter toward her, holding her tight.

Jody gasped. Over her mother's shoulder she saw Ray getting out of his truck and coming toward her. She was stunned. What was he doing there?

"That's some adventure you guys had!" Ray said jovially. "What a relief to have you back home. Safe and sound."

Beth lay on the stretcher at the admissions desk while Kate signed several papers. Lynette and Jody strode across the lobby toward them.

Lynette addressed Kate. "Kate Eastman, you probably don't remember me. My father had the grocery store. I'm Lynette Salerno, Jody's mom."

Kate nodded coolly, attempting to be polite. It was clear that she wasn't about to become best friends with Jody's mom. In fact, it looked as if she couldn't stand the sight of her or her daughter at that moment.

Jody shot Beth a worried look, mouthing, "I need to talk to you."

Lynette ignored Kate's brush off and said, "I'm so sorry. Jody should have known better. She goes to the woods all the time, but she never should have taken your daughter." She put her arm around Jody.

Beth spoke up. "You don't have to apologize. Jody didn't do anything wrong." She turned to her mother. "Hey, Mom, can Jody and I be in the same room? We just want to talk."

Kate gave Beth a look that meant, Be Quiet. Now. I Don't Want to Hear It.

Jody concurred. "Yeah, we need to talk!"

Beth saw the desperate look Jody was giving her. She couldn't understand why Jody was so freaked out, until the doors to admitting opened and Ray entered. He began to walk toward them.

Beth stared at him, speechless. Overwhelmed, she didn't know what to react to first, the fact that he was there at all, or the fact that he was about to give Jody a hug. Before she could do anything, the nurse whisked her off to the X-ray room.

Later that night, Beth was looking out from her hospital room window. She saw Jody leave with Lynette and Ray. Kate put her hands on Beth's shoulders and gently led her away from the window.

Beth was filled with confusion. What was going on? Was Jody even safe? She knew her friend had told her the truth, and her knowledge was confirmed by the phony charm in Ray's voice when he came over to hug Jody.

It was clear to Beth that Ray had known just where Jody's bruise was, because he was careful to avoid touching it when he put his arms around her. Something was fishy. She just wished she could get out of this hospital and talk to her friend.

Two days later, when the morning sun had risen high in the clear blue sky, Kate led Beth out the front doors of the hospital. She held her daughter's hand tightly, because Beth was still limping. Beth wore a cast on her right arm and a bandage on her right knee.

Kate dropped Beth's hand. "Wait here, honey. I'll get the car."

"I can make it, Mom," Beth protested.

"No, I'm going to bring the car over. Just wait." Kate was all business this morning.

"Mom, I'm not a baby."

"Oh, I see," Kate said sarcastically. "You almost get yourself killed, that makes you a grown-up."

Beth was stunned by the sharpness of Kate's tone. She did as she was told and waited for her mom to pick her up in the car.

They drove off the hospital grounds and turned onto the road. Kate had only driven a few hundred feet when she pulled the car over and burst into tears. She got out of the car and stood under the shade of a spruce tree, where she tried to control her sobs.

Beth started to get out of the car. "Please don't cry, Mom," Beth said, going over to her mother who held her tightly.

"Beth, do you have any idea what an ordeal this was for me, too?"

"It was an accident, Mom, an accident," Beth said, close to tears herself. "I'm sorry. I love you."

"I'm keeping you so far away from that girl—" began Kate.

"I can't see Jody?" Beth cried. One look at her mother's steely face and Beth knew the answer. "But Jody saved my life!"

"She almost got you killed!"

"I don't believe you're like this!" said Beth.

"All of the things I heard about Jody, I should have listened. The two of you, alone on a boat, a dangerous mountain—I thought you had better sense."

Beth was near tears again. But although her mother looked upset at her daughter's distress, she was not about to change her mind. Kate walked toward the car and got in.

Beth followed. "You have no idea what an incredible person she is. She saved me. She's a heroine."

"According to the sheriff," disagreed Kate, "your heroine doesn't seem to be able to walk into a building without stealing something."

"Does the sheriff know about the drunken fights in her house? It got so bad, Jody thought Ray was going to kill her mother."

Kate, about to launch into another protest, stopped short. "What? What are you saying?"

"When Jody tried to stop him, Ray went after her! You should see the marks on her shoulder."

Kate said nothing for awhile as she digested this information. "Ray tried to kill Lynette? But we just saw them. They—" Kate paused, began again. "Isn't Jody always lying? Why do you think she's telling the truth this time?"

Beth glared at her mother. "Because I know, Mom. I just know."

Kate shot her a look, testing her.

"It's true!" Beth insisted.

Kate watched her daughter get in the car and they drove off for home. Neither said a word the entire trip. When Kate dropped Beth off with strict instructions not to use the phone or even think of leaving the house, she went straight to the diner to meet Matt. He was waiting in a booth. She sat down and they immediately launched into a serious conversation. Their topic was Jody Salerno.

That same evening, Jody Salerno was rocking back and forth in a rocking chair in her room, filled with anxiety. It was a warm summer night and the windows of her bedroom were open. Her room was at the front of the house, adjacent to the porch, where she could see and hear Matt leaving the house with Ray and Lynette. She stopped rocking and strained to listen to what Matt had to say.

"I spoke to Judge Gould about the thefts from the school. You'll have to keep an eye on her. She can't run wild the way she used to. She's on a sort of probation, community service, under my supervision. I'm going to have her help out the school custodian."

Ray spoke next. "Well, I've tried everything I know. I hope this does her some good. What a shame."

Jody fumed. That liar! Now no one would ever believe her again. She heard Matt say goodbye to

Lynette and saw Matt walk away from the house with Ray to the sherrif's cruiser. What they said next, she couldn't make out.

Out by his cruiser, Matt spoke again to Ray. "You remember how high Frank used to toss her in the air? I never saw a kid so fearless."

"Jody's fearless, all right. The other night, the night before she caused all that trouble, you can't imagine what went on."

Matt was suddenly cautious. "Yeah, what did happen that night?"

"We caught her red-handed stealing money from her mother's wallet," Ray said. "And she looks straight at us and denies it. Then when I tell her her mother doesn't want her going off again and disappearing, that girl just lost it! She was raving and screaming. And then she picks up her fishing pole and stabs me with it. Stabs me!" He pointed to his ribs. "I couldn't believe that she did it!"

"Jeez, Ray," Matt said, shaking his head.

"Now I know why she was so set on leaving. That was the night she was going to the mountain." Ray shook his head and laughed. "Gold . . ."

Matt laughed with him. They shook hands like good buddies and Matt got in his car, heading back toward Kate's house.

When Matt arrived, Beth and Kate were out in the backyard. He told them both what had happened at Jody's house and what Ray and Lynette had told him.

"I don't believe it!" shouted Beth. "Doesn't anybody get it? He's lying!"

Kate and Matt looked startled. Beth, her splint and bandage still on, sat on a recliner, furious. She'd been moping around all day, but Kate had assumed it was the thought of wearing the bandages for the whole summer that was making Beth so crazy. Her mother didn't look like she was prepared for the force of Beth's angry reaction.

"Beth—" Kate began.

"This is just what Jody said you'd say! You twist everything around so it's all her fault!" Beth turned to Matt. "Have you seen her? Is she OK?"

"She's fine," Matt replied. "She's got plenty to do. She's going to be working at the school to make up for her stealing."

Beth shook her head. "This is incredible. Ray causes all the trouble and Jody gets punished."

"When Jody's father, Frank, died," Matt said, "the only person Lynette and Jody could count on was Ray Karnisak. Lynette went through a terrible time, and Ray got her back on her feet. There was nothing he wouldn't do for her or Jody. That's the Ray I know."

Beth stood up in a huff, overturning her chair. Limping, she stormed out of the yard along the side of the house. "He's a liar!" she yelled.

Kate looked hopelessly to Matt as they both rose to follow Beth.

Beth's face was streaked with tears. "Jody is my best friend," she said. "You can keep us apart for the rest of our lives, but nothing you say will ever change the way I feel about her. Ever!" She shot her mother and Matt a withering look and turned her back on them, as she headed up into the house.

Kate watched her go. She shivered in the warm summer night, confusion coursing through her mind. Something was not right. It wasn't like Beth to persist in a temper tantrum for no reason.

Chapter 11

Fourth of July arrived in a burst of sudden humidity, and the smell of grilled hot dogs and hamburgers hung in the air. Next door to Beth's house, a barbecue was in full swing in the Briggs's backyard.

Tracy's dad stood in front of the grill wearing a chef's hat and an apron that made him look incredibly silly, while Grace milled about with the adults, talking and laughing and serving drinks. Tracy and Samantha were huddled in a group with their friends, chatting up a storm.

Beth and Kate arrived at the gate. The splint was off Beth's arm, in its place a simple sling. Though Beth's health had improved, her spirits had not. She looked and felt like she were on her way to the gallows to be hung. She didn't want to be there. Not one bit.

Matt waved to Kate and Beth, who were being approached by Tracy and Grace.

"Hi!" said Tracy to Beth, who didn't respond.

Kate nudged Beth in the ribs. "Smile!" she ordered

her daughter under her breath.

Beth obeyed with a clearly forced, clenched smile.

Tracy noticed Beth's arm. "Oh, that's right, you got your splint off yesterday." Beth continued to ignore her.

Grace chimed in. "It's wonderful to see you looking so well, Beth."

"Thank you," Beth said grudgingly.

"C'mon," said Tracy, yanking Beth away by her good arm, "everybody's dying to talk to you."

Samantha caught sight of Tracy and Beth approaching the group of kids. "Beth!" she screeched. "How are you?"

Murmurs went up from the kids.

"Beth."

"That's Beth Eastman."

"That's the girl who . . ."

And Beth was suddenly surrounded by a crowd of curious peers. "We heard Jody almost got you killed," said Samantha.

"No, she didn't," said Beth. "I wouldn't be here if it wasn't for her."

A boy named Adam said, "Is it true that Jody had thousands of dollars of stolen equipment stashed away in a hiding place?"

"I heard it was jewelry . . ." added another kid named Doug.

"How could you go there with her?" asked some

girl Beth had never seen. "She's such a mental case!"

"She's *not* a mental case," Beth said, talking to the girl as if *she* were. "She saved my life!" Upset, Beth turned away from the kids.

From across the yard, Kate caught Beth's eye. Kate had been talking to Grace, Matt, and some other grown-ups. She looked at Beth with concern until someone pulled her back into the conversation.

Beth stood all by herself, looking out toward the woods that filled her with a sense of longing. She missed Jody. Wheaton was totally boring without her. And these other kids were idiots. She just couldn't believe how mean and how wrong they were about Jody Salerno.

Suddenly, from across the meadow, something caught her eye. Something familiar. It was a flashing light—from the sun being reflected off of a mirrorlike surface. It was Jody!

Beth smiled to herself as if the cavalry had just arrived. She was jarred back into the scene by Doug and Adam, each one holding out a plate and shoving it toward her.

"Hot dog?" said Doug, looking hopeful.

"Hamburger?" Adam said, eyeing Doug jealously. Both were competing for her attention.

Beth took both plates. She was so happy at what she'd just seen that she beamed a huge smile at the boys. Each thought the smile was meant for him, and him alone, but Beth was seeing right through them.

"Thank you," she said, moving away. "I just want to get something to drink."

"I'll get it!" said both boys at the same time.

"Really, that's OK," said Beth, smiling again. "I'll be right back." Beth slipped away and managed to lose herself in the throng of guests, purposefully avoiding where her mother and Matt stood.

Beth sneaked out of the yard, leaving the loud voices and food smells behind, and ran along the edge of the meadow toward the woods. She headed into the trees where the light had come from.

Emerging from behind a tall spruce and flashing a small compass at her was Jody.

"How ya doin', Eastman? Long time," she said.

The two girls burst into smiles, then laughter. They high-fived and gave each other a huge hug.

"I was going crazy," Beth said, breathless. "I didn't know when I'd see you again. This was the longest two weeks I've ever spent."

"I snuck out," said Jody, equally triumphant. "I gotta get back before they know I'm gone. It's like I'm under house arrest."

"Same here. It's so childish."

Jody looked at Beth intently. "You know I was

telling you the truth about Ray. I'd hate if you thought I was lying—"

Beth interrupted her. "I don't, Jody." She clasped her friend's hand. "Total trust."

"I couldn't believe my eyes when I saw him at the hospital!" Jody exclaimed.

"Tell me about it. My heart stopped. I told my mom what happened to you. But she didn't believe me. Neither did Matt." Beth felt really bad confirming Jody's worst suspicions. Adults were not to be trusted.

"They don't want to know the truth. It's easier for everyone that way," Jody said. "Actually, Ray's been kind of nice to me lately."

"No kidding!"

"He keeps asking me about the mountain. And my map. I think he wants to get the gold!"

Beth was shocked, but before she had a chance to voice her concern, Jody said, "Listen, I gotta split," and started off into the woods.

"Where are you going?" Beth asked.

"Don't you want to go back to Tracy's party?" said Jody mockingly.

"Don't get weird on me," Beth said, laughing. Jody laughed, too. "Though there are a couple of cute boys there . . ." Beth teased.

"They're just after your money," stated Jody.

"What money?"

"The money we're gonna make when we go back to the mountain and dig up Molly Morgan's treasure!" All at once, Jody freaked as if she'd seen a ghost.

Beth turned around to see what had upset Jody. It was her mother, Kate, approaching through the trees. When Beth turned back to Jody, Jody was nowhere to be found.

"I didn't mean for her to run away," said Kate to Beth, sounding sincere.

"She knows how you feel about her," said Beth, furiously marching out of the woods onto the meadow.

Kate followed her. "You can see her."

Beth stopped in her tracks. Was she hearing right? No, it couldn't be. She turned around to face her mother. "When?"

"When?" Kate was caught off guard. "Tomorrow?"

"Tomorrow?"

Kate smiled. "Tomorrow I'll drive you over."

Beth ran to her mother and made a flying leap into her arms, knocking them both off their feet and onto the grass, rolling and hugging. There was finally going to be some happiness again in the Eastman house.

The next morning, bright and early, Beth stood outside the car in the driveway honking the horn. "Mom! Come on!" she shouted to the house.

Ten minutes later, they arrived at Jody's house.

Both Kate and Beth got out of the car and walked up to the front door. Beth was filled with anticipation. She and her mother had agreed on a few ground rules the night before, and that was why Kate was there. To make sure she and Lynette agreed on the rules the two girls were going to have to live by if they were going to spend time together.

Kate knocked. No answer. The curtains were drawn. Kate knocked again, and tried the latch. The door, unlocked, opened.

"Hello?" Kate said cautiously. She took a step inside and then hesitated. "I don't like this, this isn't right," she said, backing out and shutting the door.

But Beth was undeterred. She opened the door again and entered. "Jody? Jody?" she called. And then she took a good look at the room. "Look at this!" she called in a shocked voice out to her mother. Kate followed Beth inside.

Jody's house was in total disarray. There was not one standing piece of furniture, it had all been overturned or broken. It looked to the Eastmans like the aftermath of a war. Kate and Beth moved cautiously around the room, stunned by all the damage. Smashed china tinkled under their feet as they moved inside. A broken mirror lay gaping on its side. Kate suddenly felt something tugging at her skirt. She gasped in horror and looked down.

There, sprawled on the floor, was Lynette. Her clothes were torn. Her hair was matted with blood. She had been completely battered. She held onto Kate's skirt. Then her hand dropped, and she slipped into unconsciousness.

Still unconscious, Lynette was hooked up to an IV and carried on a stretcher from the house by paramedics. Matt and his deputy, Ted, followed the paramedics out of the house. Matt went over to Beth and Kate who watched from the lawn, shaking and holding each other's hand.

"I'm going to the hospital," said Matt. "When Lynette comes out of this, maybe she'll be able to tell us where Jody is. And Ray."

Beth was anguished. Jody was in trouble, she could feel it. "I know they're going to the mountain, Matt. I'm positive!"

Kate's face registered surprise, while Matt looked a little skeptical.

Beth continued. "Ray wanted Jody to take him to the gold."

"Beth," replied Matt, "there is no gold. Everybody knows that. It's a myth."

"That's not the point!" yelled Beth, pulling her hand from Kate's. "Not if Ray thinks Jody can lead him to it!"

"Let's wait and talk to Lynette," Matt said wearily.

"You can't wait!" said Beth. "That's all you do is wait. I know what happened. Ray got drunk and told Jody to take him to the gold. Lynette must have tried to stop him, and he smashed her. Jody's in danger, and you're not doing anything!" Beth didn't know whether to scream or cry.

Kate and Matt looked at each other, overwhelmed by Beth's passionate plea.

"Matt," said Kate softly, "maybe she's right. . . ."

Matt hesitated, looking from Beth to Kate. Beth was right, it wasn't worth waiting to find out if she was right or wrong.

"Ted!" he called. The deputy rushed over. "Have the state police set up an aerial surveillance of Bear Mountain and the surrounding area. See if they can spot anything that might suggest a man and a girl are anywhere there."

The ambulance with Lynette in it pulled out, siren blaring. Matt waited for the wail to subside in the distance before he addressed Beth and Kate. "I can't believe I'm doing this," he said. "I've known Ray my whole life. Go home now. I promise, the minute I know anything, I'll call."

As Matt and Ted started off, Beth grabbed Matt's sleeve and stopped him. "Sheriff, there's something else. You've got to have a boat if you want to go to the mountain. While you go to the hospital, ask the deputy to check if any boats were stolen overnight."

Ted, impressed by Beth's gumption, turned to Matt for instructions. Matt's face showed embarrassment, but she could tell he was impressed by her grasp of the situation. Matt nodded to Ted to do as Beth suggested and the two men headed off.

"Let's go home, Beth. There's nothing more we can do," said Kate.

"No," answered Beth. "We've got to go to the hospital first."

Kate and Beth arrived at the hospital a short time later. Matt had just left Lynette's room, where still unconscious and hooked to the IV, she was being attended to by a group of nurses.

Matt walked toward Kate and Beth and ushered them back to the lobby where they could talk. "She still hasn't regained consciousness, but the doctors feel she'll pull through."

"My goodness, the poor woman," said Kate, holding Beth's shoulders tightly.

Matt's deputy, Ted, came into the lobby. "Did you hear from the state police?" asked Beth impatiently.

"They've made several passes over the mountain," he reported. "There's no sign anyone's there."

"All right, Beth?" asked Matt, glancing over at her.

"Now are you convinced?"

"That doesn't prove anything," said Beth. "They have to look *inside* the mountain, too."

Matt reacted with a rapid blinking of his eyes. She was right. Another point for the kid detective.

Ted spoke to Matt. "She was right about the stolen boat. Walter Guthrie showed up at the lake this morning to open his store—"

"His boat's gone?" Matt asked.

Ted nodded. Matt turned and smiled at Beth with a newfound respect.

"It was kind of obvious," Beth said humbly. Everyone stood up and looked at each other, then at Beth. "Let's go," she said.

They all headed out to the river near the town wharf. Walter Guthrie, a leathery old sea merchant, stood outside his dockside business: GUTHRIE'S BOAT SUPPLY. He showed Matt the post where his boat had been moored. Beth and Kate watched.

"I loved that old skiff," said Guthrie. "Fixed it up brand new."

"Was it gassed up?" asked Matt.

" 'bout two-thirds of a tank," Guthrie responded. "Don't know if this'll help you any, but I found this right where we're standing." He reached into his pocket and handed what looked like a piece of jewelry to Matt. It was a compass.

Beth reached for it. "It's Jody's. She left it for us to find—" Beth stopped.

There was dead silence in the group as the reality of the danger Jody was in finally hit the adults like a ton of bricks. Beth clutched the compass as if it were a cherished keepsake. Kate hugged her. Mother and daughter looked up as a police patrol boat reached the pier.

"I'll go out there myself, Ted. I need you to mind the harbor," said Matt, turning next to Beth. "I hope you don't mind, Beth."

"I don't mind at all," said Beth, "because I'm not staying here. I'm going with you." Before anyone could stop her, Beth leaped onto the boat.

"Get off that boat!" ordered Kate.

"Do what your mother says," agreed Matt.

"You don't know where to go inside the mountain. But I do," Beth said to Matt. "Jody showed me a passageway that takes you to the cave where she thought the gold was."

"Can't you just tell the sheriff?" Kate pleaded with her daughter. The thought of Beth leaving in another boat so soon after the accident filled her with fear.

"No. I wouldn't know how to explain it. I have to be there to show you. Come on, we're wasting time!" Beth argued.

Matt got into the boat and took the wheel, Beth at his side. Kate jumped in behind them. As the boat sped off away from the pier, each of their faces held the same look: grim determination and strength of purpose.

Chapter 12

At the helm of the police patrol boat, Matt steered into the mountain country, Kate now up front with him and her daughter. Overhead, the sound of the surveillance choppers' whirring blades cut the air, competing with the boat's motor to drown out their voices.

At the canal entrance to Bear Mountain, Matt slowed, then steered the boat into the mountain. As their eyes adjusted to the cave pool where Beth and Jody had docked Jody's boat only weeks before, they now saw a skiff secured to a stone spire. Walter Guthrie's stolen boat!

"They're here!" said Beth.

Matt switched on the boat's radio, trying to transmit through a welter of static. "Ted, can you read me? It's Matt. Send the chopper down. Walter Guthrie's boat is right here," he smiled at Beth, "just where Beth said it would be."

Beth beamed and then grabbed a flashlight, jumping off the boat onto the cave pool ridge. She secured the boat to a stone spire and started racing away along the ridge to the stairway portal.

"Beth!" screamed Kate.

Beth turned to see that Matt was still on the boat with her mother. "Come on, let's go!"

"No," said Matt firmly. "The helicopter is bringing a search and rescue team. We'll wait here for them."

"No! We can't wait!" cried Beth, moving along the ridge. "I'll show you the passageway, then I'll come back and show the other people when they get here. That way you'll be able to get a head start."

Matt paused, considering what Beth had just said. He turned to Kate, "You wait here." Before Kate could protest, Matt jumped onto the ridge and followed Beth up the stairway.

Kate felt safe in the confines of the boat for about three seconds. Then she realized she was all alone, in a dark cave, with a sinister woman- and child-beater on the loose. To top it all off, a bat came screeching past her head. Just as Beth once did, Kate ducked, grabbed an old flak jacket from the deck of the boat, and covered her head.

"No thanks!" she cried out to Matt and Beth. "I'm coming with you!"

Beth led Matt and Kate into the chamber from the stone stairway. Her mother and Matt reacted in amazement to Jody's condo, but Beth had no time to waste with explanations. While their attention was distracted by the spectacle of the underground living arrangement, Beth rushed to the ridge that extended along the wall of the chamber.

She proceeded along the ridge from the edge of the cliff floor, then up over the canal far below toward the portal high up the wall on the opposite side. When Beth was nearly all the way across, she heard her mother's voice.

"No! Beth, come back."

"It's OK. I'm just showing the sheriff," said Beth, pointing to the portal. "That's where you go."

"All right, Beth, I see it," said Matt. "Now come back here."

But Beth ignored him and continued forward. She reached the other side of the chamber, just a few steps away from the portal to the passageway.

"Beth! Stop!" called Kate.

Beth paused. "Matt, you come with me. Mom, you go down to the entrance, then when the rescue people get here, show them the way. Jody saved my life, I save hers. That's how it is!" she exclaimed. Then she ducked into the portal and was engulfed by darkness.

"Do what she says," said Matt to Kate. He had to catch up to her before they all got lost. "Don't worry, I'll go with her."

The curving portal was dark and narrow. There was enough room to squeeze through one body at a time, and that was about it. With the flashlight beam guiding her, Beth scooted up a curving incline, dodging stalactites that constantly threatened to hit her in the face. She turned left, then right, taking curve after curve as fast as she could go on her sore knee. Behind her, Matt's footsteps echoed far away.

"Beth! Eth-eth-eth!" she heard Matt call. "Answer so I know you're there-ere-ere-ere!"

Beth stopped at a fork in the tunnel. The passageway branched off to two separate paths. "I'm waiting!" she called back behind her to reassure Matt. Why was he taking so long? They had to find Jody, and fast!

Huffing and puffing around a curve, nearly ready to drop from exhaustion from the uphill path and the rapid ascent of the girl he was following, came Matt.

"You look awful!" Beth said.

"How nice of you," Matt quipped, trying to catch his breath. He caught sight of the fork in the road. "Which way do we go?"

"I don't know," stated Beth with a sigh, scouring the area for clues.

"What do you mean? I thought you said Jody showed you!"

"You need a map to find your way once you're inside," answered Beth.

"Where's the map?" asked Matt, knowing at once that he wasn't going to like the answer.

"Ray must have it."

"Oh. Great!"

"Look!" Beth said triumphantly. She had discovered a trail of footprints leading into the left passageway. "Aren't those footprints?" she asked.

Matt crouched down to examine the cave floor. "Yes. They weren't made that long ago."

That was all Beth needed to hear. She ducked into the cave on the left and pressed forward. It was uphill all the way. As she was about to disappear around a curve, Matt said from a ways behind her, "Would you wait a second?" He finally managed to catch up to her, still winded.

"Don't they make you guys exercise?" she demanded with a smirk.

Matt gave her a warning look. Beth proceeded, finding more footprints. And more curves—all uphill. The ascending curves finally leveled off abruptly and fed into a stone corridor. The incline was noticeably less severe.

"Thank goodness," said Matt, head down trying to avoid bumping it against the ceiling.

Ahead of him, about halfway down the tunnel, Beth suddenly paused. "Oh no!" she said, her voice filled with real fear.

Matt reacted. "What is it?" he asked. When he caught up to Beth he saw what the problem was quite clearly. Caught in the flashlight beam, about ten yards up the corridor, was a huge chasm in the ground. It was at least six feet wide. But from the distance where they stood, it was impossible to tell how big the drop was in between the two far-apart edges. There was no other way to get across.

All at once, Beth took a deep breath and with the whoosh of an Olympic sprinter, she dashed right toward the chasm!

"Oh my . . . Oh no, Beth, oh no, please don't, for the love of—"

In a burst of speed, Beth reached the chasm and, holding her breath, leaped across to the other side, where she landed safely on her feet.

Matt looked like he was about to have a heart attack. "Are you out of your mind? How could you even think of doing that?" he screamed at Beth, not sure whether to be angry at her for trying or impressed with her for succeeding.

"It was easy," said Beth. "Now it's your turn."

Matt did not look happy. Summoning all his nerve, he filled up his chest with air, took a running start, and headed for the chasm. In a lumbering, long, slow-motion movement, he managed to clear the space and land on his feet. But the weight of his body tipped him backward, and he was losing his balance. Beth grabbed his shirt and pulled him forward to safety.

"Whew!" said Matt, thanking Beth with his eyes and his grateful smile.

"Nice jump," she said.

Off they went again. Around and around the curving caves. Unexpectedly they came to a major dilemma. Captured in the glow of the flashlight, the cave split off into five different caves. And there were no more footprints to follow since the ground beneath them had turned into hard rock. The entrances to each of the caves were hard rock, as well, indicating that having the luxury of following footprints was now over.

"No more footprints," said Matt, stating what they both already knew. "This is all solid rock."

Beth swept the flashlight beam over the caves. "Look!" On the wall, just outside the entrance to one of the caves was a crudely drawn arrow scratched into the stone with a rock.

"Thank you, Jody!" said Beth.

She and Matt hopped into the cave, rushing down and up, then twisting and descending and ascending into the cave. Beth was in the lead as usual, when she stopped abruptly. Her eyes widened with hope, and she gasped. A faint glimmer of a smile appeared at the corners of her mouth.

Some distance behind her, Matt could tell that she had stopped. "What? Another surprise?" Matt said, reaching her and seeing her hopeful expression.

Beth held the flashlight up to Matt's face. The bulb was off. "I switched it off," Beth said.

"Then where's the light coming from?" he asked.

"Exactly!" said Beth. She and Matt both turned in the direction of the light in front of them and raced forward, taking the next few curves with all the speed they could manage, until they were stopped in their tracks by a brightly lit passageway that intersected the cave. They looked right to see sunlight flooding in through the entrance to the passageway on the face of the mountain.

To their left was a dusky, moss-covered, and utterly astonishing sight. This cave was like a funhouse from another planet. Hundreds upon hundreds of razor-thin slivers of light flickered in through cracks on both sides of the corridor. Beams of natural light bounced off of Beth, making her look like a moving disco ball.

"This is awesome!" she cried. She ran down the dusky passageway, crossing interlocking short corridors slashed by thin rays of light. Suddenly she realized that she couldn't hear Matt's footsteps behind her anymore. She was alone. And suddenly she *felt* very alone. It was creepy.

"Matt?!"

"Where are you?" she heard faintly from a distance.

"Here!" she called.

"Where is here?"

"I don't know!" cried Beth, filled with a sharp sense of panic. Beth ran helplessly through the maze, trying to find her way back to Matt. "Matt? Matt!" She was lost. There was no answer. She paused, trying to retrace her steps in her mind and then setting off to do it with her feet. She began to run, in circles it seemed. "Matt?" No answer. She ran in the opposite direction, aimlessly, frightened, and collided head-first with something. Somebody?

They both gasped. It was Jody! The girls were so stunned that they stared at each other in utter silence. Then they burst into laughter that for Jody soon turned into terrible, wrenching sobs.

Beth couldn't tell whether it was joy, relief, anguish, or what. The girls hugged, and Beth, too, began to cry.

"I did it, Jody! I made it!"

"City girl . . ." whispered Jody in between sobs.

"I wasn't sure I could do it. So I pretended I was you. Because you're the bravest person I know." Beth looked at Jody, who smiled, but did not reply, her racking sobs continued. Beth studied at her friend closely. Jody seemed OK on the outside, but her whole body was shaking. Beth gripped her by the shoulders.

"Take a deep breath," she instructed. Jody gulped in air. "Again. And again. Keep doing it." Jody obeyed. "Be strong—like Molly!"

Jody took more gulps of air and her sobs slowly subsided. She looked numb to Beth, totally drained of all energy and momentum.

"Where's Ray?" Beth asked gently.

Jody tried to get the words out, at first failing. Then she said, "He's back there somewhere. He's drunk and he's crazy. He can't find the gold. I got away. I ran. I just kept running." Jody gestured behind her, to the maze of the cavern.

"He's probably lost," said Beth. "Good."

"My mother? Do you know if she's OK? When we left, I couldn't tell, I couldn't tell, Beth!" Jody began to gulp in air again.

"She'll be fine," Beth said, touching her arm. "They're taking care of her in the hospital."

Through a mask of tears, Jody tried to tell her what had happened. "He took my map, then he said I had to go with him. She tried to stop him with my father's gun, but he grabbed it away from her and hit her with it. She tried so hard to stop him."

"I know," Beth said. "Let's go, Jody. Let's find our way out of here." She took Jody's hand and began leading her through the maze. Unlike their first trek into these mountains, Beth realized that this time she,

Beth, would have to be the fearless leader.

"Matt's here somewhere," said Beth. "And a rescue squad also is coming for us. Jody, I know we're going to be all right."

Beth could see that Jody took visible comfort from Beth's words and reassuring manner. But Beth started to look troubled as each corridor lead into another corridor—until they seemed to be going in circles. Again.

"Do you have any idea which way we should go?" asked Beth.

"Beth! The gold!" cried Jody.

Beth looked where Jody was pointing to. There was a brilliant pool of light shooting out of the cave wall just ahead. They burrowed excitedly through the boulders on the wall, loosening them and opening them up to a spectacular flood of light.

The light was so bright that at first the girls had to cover their eyes. The color of the glow was golden! Just like it was the day of the solstice. Beth and Jody looked through the opening of the wall directly into an adjacent chamber where a grotto was hidden.

Once inside they gawked at the huge spherical cave, the center ring of a circle of stalagmites that climbed from the ground as high up as sixty feet! A curtain of stalactites draped from the domed roof, reaching almost to the ground. The yellowy golden glow was everywhere. It looked like a planetarium filled with millions of stars.

"Molly Morgan's fortress of gold," said Jody.

"It's all true!"

Beth and Jody waded a few steps into the golden lake at the center of the chamber. They burst into smiles as they saw their bodies take on the radiant glow from above.

"You were right, Jody!" exclaimed Beth.

"I always knew it. . . ."

"It's ours, it all belongs to us!" cried Beth in joy. She dove into the lake and swam across the water to the bank under the lowest part of the dome. "I can't wait to grab some!"

Jody remained near the entrance, still dazed and tired from her ordeal with Ray. She took pleasure in watching her friend swim for the gold.

Beth reached the low rim of the dome and grabbed a handful of the starlike specks. She cringed. "Yechhh!" she said angrily. "These are worms!"

"What?" said Jody.

"Worms! Glow worms!" said Beth.

"That's impossible!" cried Jody.

"The light we saw, it wasn't gold, it's millions of glow worms!" Beth disgustedly shook her hand free of the golden creepy crawlers. Leechlike glow worms stuck to her skin and hair. She shivered as she picked off the last of the worms from her clothes.

"It can't be," protested Jody. "Maybe the gold's under the water—" Jody reached under the surface, and retrieved a handful of mud. She quickly scraped it off, frustrated.

Beth looked suddenly horror-stricken as a figure burst into the blinding light behind Jody like a monstrous apparition. It grabbed Jody. Ray!

"Jody!" screamed Beth.

Beth's cry startled Ray and caught him completely off guard. His gun went off. It hit the stalactite above Beth. She dove beneath some rocks.

Unable to talk or breathe, Jody fought to escape the vicelike grip of Ray's arm clamped around her throat, as he dragged her toward the golden glow of the water. In his other hand was the gun.

"Look at this!" he cried, his voice deep and gnarled. "I found it!" Dazzled, in a slow-motion drunken daze, he let go of Jody and reached down to gather up handfuls of the gold.

"Worms? Glow worms?" his accusing voice screeched into the cave walls, echoing back furiously. He turned to Jody and lurched in her direction. "You've been nothing but trouble since the day you were born!"

Ray grabbed Jody. But from out of the shadows, a mining shovel came crashing down on his head. Blinded by the light of the grotto, neither Beth nor

Jody could see who, behind the sheath of light, was holding the shovel.

Ray staggered. Another blow came crashing down onto his back. Ray gasped, disoriented, and Jody slumped like a rag doll, disappearing into the light. Ray went after Jody and his attacker—all of them now obscured to Beth's view by the blinding light.

Beth dove into the lake and swam across, staring into the blaze of light and hearing the sounds of a fight. Huge shadows on the cave wall showed two adult-sized figures grappling for the gun, then Ray's attacker slammed him decisively with the shovel. The gun skidded out of the light and across the bank.

Ray staggered forward out of the light and fell, breathing heavily, badly bruised.

Beth finally saw Jody. She was being carried out of the light in the arms of a mysterious woman. Beth splashed onto the bank where the woman gently set Jody down.

Beth and Jody stared at her. The woman had saved their lives! She looked like an ancient sorceress or a prophet out of the Bible. Her eyes had the glint and strength of diamonds. Her withered, parchmentlike skin burnished with gold under the glow of the dome. She was tall and imposing, a woman of power, beauty, and magic.

Jody rose on shaky legs and gazed at her as one

would upon a priestess. "Molly?" asked Jody, whispering in awe.

The woman simply stood there, then slowly backed into the blinding light at the entrance. Suddenly Matt rushed in, followed by other people from the rescue squad. The girls turned away from the woman to Matt.

Matt grabbed the gun from the ground, rushing to Jody and Beth and wrapping them up in his arms. He then noticed the glow as if for the first time. "Gold?" Beth and Jody shook their heads, no. "But we found her—Molly Morgan—she's here!"

Jody and Beth turned to look back at where the mysterious woman was. But she wasn't there. She was gone. The two girls rushed through the light to follow her and emerged into the adjacent cave corridor. The woman was nowhere to be seen. She was simply and finally gone.

Back in the grotto, Matt walked over to that sorry specimen of a man that he'd known since they were both boys. Matt and Ray faced each other.

Ray laughed, shaking his head. "You believe that kid? She wanted to look for gold. I told her no, but you just can't argue with her. So I thought she'd be safer if I came along."

Matt nodded toward the gun in his own hand. "What's this for? Safety?"

"Well, sure," Ray said, stumbling over his words. "Who knows who you could run into here?" Ray saw that Matt was not buying it. "Hey, Matt, this is Ray. You're looking at me like you don't know me."

Matt turned away from Ray in disgust and pity as Ray was led out in handcuffs. Matt looked for Beth and Jody, but a nearby rescue worker told him they had already headed out of the cave back to the outside of Bear Mountain.

Chapter 13

Beth and Jody searched the cave outside the grotto for the mysterious woman. But they could find no trace of her in any of the caves. When they finally emerged into the blinding sunlight outside Bear Mountain, the whole episode seemed almost as unreal as the fortress of golden glow worms.

The entire way home on the police patrol boat, they argued about whether the woman was Molly Morgan or not. Jody insisted that it had to have been her. Beth argued that Molly could never have lived for nearly seventy years hidden in a cave. Back and forth they fought, delighted to have each other safe and sound to fight with in the first place.

When Beth, Kate, and Matt accompanied Jody to the hospital to see her mother, it was a reunion none of them would ever forget. Jody rushed into the sun-filled hospital room and would have jumped into the bed atop her mother had Matt not reminded her of her mother's injuries.

Lynette's hand trembled when she reached out and touched her beloved daughter's arm and then folded her into a warm embrace. The Eastmans watched from the doorway, overcome with emotion.

When Matt walked them down the hospital corridor, both of his arms around an Eastman woman, Beth suddenly felt like she had a whole family again. It felt good. In fact, it felt just right: warm, safe, and whole.

But the most unforgettable day of Jody and Beth's lives was actually a few months following their ordeal in the cave.

"Beth! Jody!" Matt called out to the girls across the meadow in front of Beth's house. He was rushing toward them.

Kate and Lynette were watching from a picnic blanket. Jody had stayed with the Eastmans all summer while Lynette recovered. With Jody's help, Lynette had stayed away from alochol and was in a program that taught her how to stay away from it for good. In her newfound sobriety, Lynette was able to be the mother she had always wanted to be. Jody, wary at first, had grown to trust and love Lynette deeply. Jody finally had the relationship with her mother that she had always secretly wished for. As for Lynette's emotional scars from Ray, those took the longest to heal, but finally Lynette came home to Jody for good.

And that was the day that found Matt eagerly beckoning to all four of them from the edge of the meadow. Jody and Lynette, Kate and Beth ran to meet him.

Matt could barely speak, he was so breathless. "There's someone in my office who wants to talk to Jody and Beth. Someone very important!"

Jody turned excitedly to Beth. "I knew it, I knew it!" she exclaimed.

"Knew what?" Beth asked.

"I don't know, but I just knew it!" Jody replied mysteriously.

They all drove to the police station in Matt's car. The siren was not on, but Matt had the red and blue lights flashing because of the urgency of the matter. The girls and their mothers were intrigued.

Everyone rushed toward the entrance, all noticing the brand new Jaguar luxury car parked in front and the crowds of townspeople, including Tracy and Samantha, dying of curiosity. An armored bank truck was parked behind the Jaguar.

Two security guards emerged from the truck, each carrying a bulging sack and followed Beth and Jody inside the police station.

As they entered the building, a distinguished, well-dressed gentleman rose and extended his hand to shake each of theirs.

"Girls," said Matt, "this is Everett Graham."

"You are Jody and you are Beth," he said to them, identifying both of them correctly. "I recognize you both. I couldn't turn on the television for weeks without seeing you."

Graham and the girls shook hands. The guards remained inside the entrance. Behind them, Tracy, Samantha, and the townspeople had their noses pressed against the window, trying desperately to catch a glimpse of what was going on.

"These are the girls' mothers, Mrs. Salerno and Mrs. Eastman," said Matt.

Graham smiled and shook their hands, too. Then he moved to the desk and placed his briefcase on top of it. "Well, let me tell you why I'm here," he began. "I'm an attorney and I represent a client who wishes to remain anonymous." He snapped open the briefcase with a loud click. "My client wishes to present a gift to Ms. Beth Eastman and Ms. Jody Salerno. Will you please sign this document to acknowledge receipt of the gift?"

Just as the girls were about to sign, the security guards placed the two sacks in front of them. Jody and Beth gulped and stared at the sacks, then hurriedly signed the document, pens flying.

"Congratulations, young ladies," said Graham, indicating the sacks with a flourish.

A hush fell over the room. Everyone gathered around as Beth and Jody opened the sacks and looked inside. Their eyes bulged out in surprise. They spilled the contents of the sacks onto the desk. Magnificent, radiant, gold nuggets caught the light with dazzling brilliance. The value of the gold had been appraised at two million dollars!

Beth looked at Jody with her mouth open. Jody's face beamed. Jody glanced out the window at the crowds of townspeople, their faces registering shock. All those years that Jody had suffered from their mean spiritedness flashed across her face—and then seemed to melt away. She had believed in a dream that most people would never have the courage to believe in, much less follow, and it had come true. Her mother was finally well, and now she, Jody Salerno, was wealthy. More than wealthy, she was rich! Jody gave a little smile of triumph toward the townspeople and looked back down at her treasure. It sparkled and gleamed right back at her.

That evening, against the glowing light of a brilliant sunset on Bear Mountain, Jody and Beth slapped a loud high-five.

Who was their mysterious benefactor? They fought about it the entire way up to the mountain—and all the way back down.

Jody swore it was the woman who saved them, Molly Morgan. But was the woman really Molly? argued Beth. They'd never know for sure. But they both knew that they'd probably be arguing about it for the rest of their lives.

And they did. Even as grown-up best friends with daughters of their own, they could never settle on that one issue. But the one thing they did agree on was that dreams were very important and that above all else, friendship was the most precious treasure in the world. Beth and Jody both passed on these wisdoms to their girls. Over and over again they told their daughters the story of Molly Morgan and the fortress of gold. Soon, their children could recite it by heart. That was just fine with Beth and Jody, for now they both knew that their adventure would live on forever.